Deadly Murder

ANGUS BRODIE AND MIKAELA FORSYTHE MURDER MYSTERY
BOOK FOURTEEN

CARLA SIMPSON

Prologue

NOVEMBER 1893, WHITE'S GENTLEMAN'S
CLUB, ST. JAMES'S STREET, LONDON

YOUNG LORD SALISBERY pushed his hand back through his hair and restored his disheveled appearance with a lopsided grin as he made his way past the entrance of the card room and waved to those still at the tables. He then made his way somewhat unsteadily down the central staircase to the front hall of the club.

It was near three in the morning, and he'd been there since the early evening, gambling at cards. He then bet on who could finish a decanter of brandy first. Along with another bet when the first rain of the night might fall. He had lost that bet by an hour's time. And then took himself, along with another decanter of brandy to a chorus of crude remarks, up to that private third story chamber where another sort of game awaited.

She was experienced and might have been twenty or thirty. It didn't matter. She wore a costume and a mask, her dark hair loose about her shoulders.

Others had spoken of her talents. No need for the usual drugs, she was creative and willing.

It didn't bother him that others had been with her, it made the liaison all the more exciting. Equally exciting as the rumor that she was a well-known member of society. Hence the mask, which remained as she removed everything else she wore.

The raucous cheers of the others faded as he reached the main floor hall with that gallery of portraits on the walls that included esteemed members past and present, including the portrait of his own father.

He'd requested a coach as he left that third floor chamber, the footman at the club disappearing ahead of him to make certain it was done.

After all, he could hardly use a coach with his family crest to return to his townhouse. The neighbors would surely gossip regarding his late—or rather early morning return, depending on how one looked at it, and the fourth night this week. That would certainly bring on a lecture from his father.

He gave a mocking salute to the man in that portrait as he carefully guided his footsteps toward the main entrance.

The doorman greeted him. "A coach awaits you, sir."

He nodded, then descended the steps to the waiting coach. One of the club's footmen held the door open for him and he almost made it inside without assistance.

Young Salisbery laughed, the effects of brandy and other enjoyments still there as he finally seated himself and gazed across the inside of the coach. He gradually focused on the figure seated there in the shadows.

"Oh, very well," he said with an alcoholic chuckle as the coach moved off. "We shall share as long as you are going the same direction."

Another chuckle turned to a sudden gasp as the light from the streetlamp they passed flashed on the blade of a knife.

It was quickly done, so quick that Salisbery stared with

surprise, then disbelief at the front of his linen shirt as a dark stain slowly spread. He looked up through an alcoholic haze as he realized what had just happened. He tried to speak, but no words came out, only a startled gasp as he stared at that figure who sat across from him.

His guest tapped on the roof of the coach. It slowly rolled to a stop. His fellow passenger stepped down onto the cobbled street, then closed the door.

A nod to the driver and the coach moved on.

Young Lord Salisbery slumped against the seat of the coach, staring sightlessly into the night, an envelope left behind, tucked in his dying hand...

One

#204 THE STRAND, LONDON

I STEPPED DOWN from the coach upon our arrival at the office, somewhat gingerly. That cautious step, however, was quite enough to set the pounding at the back of my head off once more as the tall, dark-eyed man beside me gently clasped my arm.

"Are ye all right?" Brodie asked with more than a little amusement as he stepped away to pay the driver.

"Of course," I assured him, not about to let on that I was suffering somewhat from the previous evening, the birthday celebration that I shared with my great aunt.

Aunt Antonia has always considered it quite remarkable that we were born on the same day, November 9th, albeit sixty years apart. That number—sixty—I am sworn not to reveal.

She had adopted a scheme several years before, for when she became a year older, she simply chose to subtract two years if anyone asked. She had been using that scheme for so long that in no time at all, it would put her at my age sometime in the future.

"We shall be twins!" she had exclaimed when I pointed that out. "How marvelous!"

In that regard, it did seem as if it would be necessary to postpone her final voyage in a Viking longboat until well into the next century, a delay I approved of most heartily.

I adored her, and it did seem that we were much alike in temperament according to our horoscope.

"Twins?" Brodie exclaimed when I explained her method for calculating her age. "The world is no longer safe."

I had to agree.

Most certainly, she did not appear anywhere near eighty-seven years, while, at the moment, I felt every one of my own twenty-seven years.

I had indulged a bit the night before over tarot readings, board games, charades, and crambo, a word rhyming game that became quite colorful, even risqué, as the evening continued. My great-aunt had also arranged for a magician to the entertainment of all in attendance.

While my sister and her husband had departed early, Brodie and I had remained quite late.

He had never experienced that sort of celebration and I had caught him watching from across the great hall with his good friend, Munro, each with a glass of Old Lodge whisky.

It could be said that I had no clear memory of the coach ride to the townhouse at the end of the evening, nor the fact that Brodie had put me to bed, although he had reminded me of it this morning over breakfast.

"Ye were not completely honest with me about yer nightly habits," he had commented over very strong coffee.

I had no idea what he was talking about and did not ask. It was not necessary as he was most forthcoming with one corner of his mouth lifted in amusement.

"Ye snore when ye're blottered."

That was undoubtedly one of those Scottish words that needed no translation under the circumstances, and an obvious reference to my celebratory condition the previous evening.

"I do not snore," I corrected him, between my housekeeper's trips from the kitchen to dining room with our breakfast.

"You do, miss, if I may say so," Mrs. Ryan added. "But only when you've had a bit of the drink." To which she refilled my cup with more coffee.

Mrs. Ryan and I had shared the loss of her daughter in our first inquiry case. Mary Ryan had been my sister's maid, a bright young woman with a keen sense of humor. She had disappeared along with my sister and was tragically murdered.

In the time since, Mrs. Ryan had become my housekeeper and far more. Much like a surrogate for the mother that I had lost early on, in the way she looked after me. At least most of the time, in spite of her present comment.

That brought a devilish grin from Brodie.

"It seems that ye might have also wakened Mrs. Ryan with the noise ye made. And I will add that ye were quite insistent in other matters as well," he added as she returned to the kitchen. "If I was not an understanding sort, I might have been embarrassed."

Brodie embarrassed?

I sincerely doubted that it had ever occurred. I did have a very clear memory regarding what he was speaking of, however I would not give him the satisfaction of acknowledging it.

"I have no idea what you are talking about."

Which brought us to the office somewhat late in the morning, with me struggling somewhat from the effects of the previous evening. For which I fully understood the reasons some women were "indisposed" the day after such celebrations.

However, I was not the sort to be indisposed, providing I could navigate the stairs to the office on the second-floor landing without a mishap.

For his part, Brodie was quite cheerful. Aggravatingly so.

"A bit of the hair of the dog is in order," he said.

One of those sayings that made no sense as he kept a firm hand on my arm and we climbed the stairs together, my other hand on the stair rail.

The *"hair of the dog,"* as it turned out, was a dram of my aunt's very fine whisky which he poured and set before me on the table in the office. And since it was very near midday, I did not argue the matter.

"And then more coffee," he added.

He was most definitely enjoying my condition far too much as the dear man proceeded to set the pot on the iron stove.

"Hair of the dog, I assume that is a Scottish phrase?" I said after my second sip and had to admit that it was easing my "wobbles" as he called them.

"Well known among all those who spend time in taverns and pubs and over-indulge on a dare," he added pointedly.

"I am convinced Aunt Antonia cheated," I insisted.

"Is that so?"

"Absolutely."

He had stepped into the adjoining bedroom and returned with a folded cloth that he'd obviously soaked in water.

"Hold this against yer head."

"It's cold," I pointed out.

"Aye, hot water is not yet available with the improvements." He pressed the cloth against my forehead, then added my hand over it as I sat at my desk.

"And I do not snore," I emphatically informed him.

"Nor make demands on the man ye keep company with?" he added.

"You seem quite well recovered," I pointed out.

"There was a moment when I was in fear for my life."

I burst out laughing and immediately regretted it at the pain that shot through my head.

"I shall be more considerate in the future," I replied and wondered if all married couples had such conversations.

"Please, do not be. It was most interesting."

"For someone who thought he had nothing more to learn regarding such things between a man and woman?" I inquired.

"Interesting in the manner in which ye learned such things."

I ignored that. He could be such a devil.

As the dram steadied me and the coffee cleared my head, I went through the mail that had been delivered earlier.

"There is an envelope from Mr. Peterson." I handed it to Brodie.

We had just concluded a case for the man regarding missing payroll from a recent deposit for his trading company.

It had been resolved after questioning bank staff where the substantially reduced payroll deposit was made.

When Brodie was able to determine that there was no involvement by the bank clerk, he then questioned Mr. Peterson's son who had been tasked with delivering the payroll to the bank.

Brodie was able to trip the young man up over his excuses which were quite inventive and then proceeded to retrieve a gaming ticket from the location where it had been hidden—in the heel of the young man's boot. It did seem as if Brodie might have used that particular hiding place himself at one time.

Young Mr. Peterson had stopped over at a well-known gaming parlor on his way to the bank. Usually quite lucky in such things and not his first time—it seemed that he usually won enough to cover his bets.

However, in this particular instance, he had lost a considerable portion of the week's payroll. He had hoped to disguise the loss by claiming that the number amount written on the accompanying deposit ticket from the warehouse manager was incorrect.

However...never attempt to outwit someone who has perhaps used every scheme possible in his past life on the streets, not to mention that experience with the Metropolitan Police.

Brodie opened the envelope.

"Our fee for solving the case of the missing payroll," he commented as he handed me a bank cheque.

I had been doubtful there would be payment considering the thief turned out to be the client's son, resulting in the usual reprimand for the young man and then the obvious effort to simply move past the issue.

Somewhat surprisingly, Mr. Peterson paid our fee in full, along with an additional amount for our discretion in the matter and a note of gratitude.

"You seem to have made an impression on the man," I commented.

"Not so much Mr. Peterson as his son, when I reminded him where thieves usually ended up."

"From experience, I would imagine."

There was a shrug beneath the cut of Brodie's coat.

"When ye've been places and can share what it is like, it might leave an impression."

"It is possible that it was enough of an impression that young Mr. Peterson won't be inclined to steal again."

"Aye, that and the threat from his father to turn him out without a farthing to his name."

The service bell rang out on the landing, a situation soon to be enhanced with the installation of the new lift that was presently a work in progress.

Brodie went out onto the landing and then down the stairs. He quickly returned with an envelope in hand. It was unmarked except for our names on the outside and noticeably without a return address or name of who had sent it.

"This was delivered by the courier service."

Most intriguing, I thought, as he opened it, read the contents, and then handed it to me.

It appeared that we were being summoned, albeit politely, to a private meeting at The Grand Hotel, at a specific suite of rooms that I was *somewhat* familiar with at three o'clock that same afternoon...

WE WAITED in the drawing room of that private suite at The Grand Hotel, a suite that "*didn't exist*" according to hotel staff if one inquired, after receiving what might be called a royal summons that had been simply signed, A.E.

I was familiar with those initials that I had seen at the conclusion of our first inquiry case. A.E., Albert Edward, Prince of Wales.

"*We*" referred to both Brodie and myself, according to an agreement that neither of us would undertake *separate* cases after a particular situation that could have ended badly. Although, I did have it well in hand by the time he had arrived.

Over the intervening months, there had been the odd case or two, including the Peterson case, with most of our time devoted to the changes we wanted to make to the office now that Brodie was the official owner of the building on The Strand. Such as the lift we were having installed to assist those for whom the stairs presented a difficulty.

I originally thought of Mr. Cavendish, who assisted us from time to time in our inquiries, while Brodie had pointed out that it might be convenient for my great aunt, who made frequent visits when she was out and about in her motor carriage.

The lift was to be powered by electricity and was very nearly completed, along with an expansion of the second-floor loo, repairs to the ground floor shop at #104 that had stood empty for some time, and then a remodel project of the third floor.

Brodie had decided to let out the ground floor shop to a business prospect. He was determined that ownership of the building should include rental income from the other spaces.

The third floor, which had been vacant for some time, needed a great amount of work. My great aunt had ideas about that. I could only imagine what that might include.

Brodie had left Mr. Cavendish in charge of the final test for the lift that we had to postpone after the arrival of our *"unofficial"* summons, delivered by one of the courier services about London.

It was quite odd that His Royal Highness had chosen one of those services about London rather than the official royal courier. So here we were, awaiting the arrival of the Prince of Wales.

I was familiar with the suite of rooms at The Grand as I had been there before with my good friend, Templeton, who at the time was rumored to be the *'theatre companion'* of the Prince of Wales.

That particular title was subject to various interpretations that included mistress and lover although she had vehemently denied it at the time.

"Dear Bertie and I are just...very good friends."

Good friends, my foot.

I did like Templeton very much, a well-traveled, independent woman much like myself. We got along without any pretenses and shared a colorful conversation from time to time. And then there was her pet iguana, Ziggy, who was now in residence at the London Zoo.

She was forever attempting to persuade me to join her on her next tour to the United States. However, that had been pre-empted by the man who presently paced the floor of the suite.

"How am I supposed to greet the man?" Brodie asked with a frown. "I canna exactly slap him on the back and offer to buy him a pint," he said with more than a little sarcasm.

"Aside from the slap on the back, you might simply say— 'Good afternoon, Your Highness,'" I suggested as I stood and straightened his tie. "And then let him provide the reason for the meeting. It isn't as if you haven't met before," I pointed out.

Their past acquaintance had been cordial, without the usual formalities required when speaking to a royal. Yet, that might have had to do with the fact that Brodie had just saved the man's life and those of his family.

"And no official courier. Most interesting," Brodie commented.

It was then that I heard the door to the suite open, and His Royal Highness, Albert Edward, the Prince of Wales, and future King of England, entered the room.

"It seems that we are about to learn the reason," I commented.

The Prince of Wales was dressed surprisingly informal in trousers and jacket, although of the finest quality, that might have been worn for a day out sporting or at his hunting lodge. He had cap in hand; his other hand extended to Brodie in greeting in that casual way between men that immediately emphasized that this was not an "official" meeting.

No personal staff accompanied him, no equerry, nor Sir Knollys, his private secretary. Not even a footman.

"I appreciate you meeting with me on such short notice, Mr. Brodie," the Prince of Wales greeted him.

"Of course," Brodie replied, obviously surprised by HRH's casual deportment.

His Highness turned to me. "And Lady Forsythe. Always a pleasure."

I was not into curtsies and nodded an acknowledgement.

"Your Highness."

"Let us dispense with the formalities, please," he told me, his expression quite serious.

"Shall we begin then?" Brodie replied with a gesture to the overstuffed settee and two side chairs that sat before the fireplace.

His Highness nodded and sat on the settee. Brodie and I each took a chair across from him.

"I have not forgotten your service in the past on behalf of myself and my family, Mr. Brodie. And Lady Forsythe, of course, who was injured at the time. A most dangerous situation and handled with amazing skill and...discretion.

"It is in that regard that I sent that note myself while out and about and not officially, if you get my meaning."

Brodie nodded.

"There is a matter that has arisen that is somewhat alarming as well as perplexing and needs immediate attention." He seemed most serious as he continued.

"I assure you that it is not what you might assume from past rumors about certain...indiscretions," he added without elaborating. There was no need as they were well known, and it was the only reference he made to several rather famous well-known affairs. The man did have a fondness not only for actresses but a titled lady or two.

"It does seem as though the man cannot keep his trousers buttoned," my great aunt had remarked quite bluntly when one particular affair became known.

"And then there was that nonsense about a chair or some other piece of furniture."

I did appreciate that she hadn't elaborated on that particular subject.

"I much prefer a rogue to a nobleman," she had continued at the time. *"It does add excitement, wouldn't you agree, dear?"*

I looked over at Brodie. I had to admit that I did agree on that.

His Highness stood then and paced across the room.

"I must ask for your discretion once more, of course, in the interest of a valued friend, until the purpose behind this is determined."

Brodie nodded once more.

"Of course," I replied.

"You must be aware of a situation, in the matter of the death of a young man, the son of Lord Salisbery, the month past."

"A matter of a robbery after leaving his club late of the night almost six weeks ago," Brodie commented.

"So, it would seem, according to the newspapers and what the Metropolitan Police have determined," His Royal Highness added.

"However..." He reached inside his jacket and retrieved what appeared to be a badly stained envelope. He crossed the suite and handed it to Brodie.

"This was found by Lord Salisbery's footman in the young

man's hand when the coach arrived at their residence and his body was discovered."

Brodie unfolded the stationary, read the contents, then handed it to me.

"The sins of the father will be visited upon the children...?" A biblical saying, if I was correct, and quite cryptic.

"Have the police seen this?" Brodie inquired.

There was a pause. "Lord Salisbery has not shown it to anyone else as yet."

"It could be helpful in finding the murderer..." Brodie pointed out.

"That is the reason your assistance is being requested," HRH replied. "It is well known that in your own search for Lady Forsythe's sister, your services were acquired to great success. And you are sensitive to the need to avoid the sensationalism that usually accompanies such a situation."

I was well aware of that and there was no need for his reminder of it. And it was no secret that the dailies feasted on any information, real or otherwise, about those in certain circles.

That had not been my concern when my sister disappeared. The concern had been the delays and lack of attention it was given by Chief Inspector Abberline, who had referred to her disappearance more than once as a lady of means who had simply taken herself off, even with the "unfortunate circumstances" of her maid's death.

I caught the subtle change of Brodie's expression. He was not one to turn away someone in a dire situation, still I had learned to read his expressions. He was not pleased to be called into a situation where a valuable piece of information had been withheld from the investigation.

"With all due respect, sir, this might be a situation better suited to the Agency," he diplomatically replied.

However, I caught the look of consternation in the expression on HRH's face.

"I appreciate your candor, Mr. Brodie. However, I am personally requesting your expertise in the matter. I want you and Lady Forsythe to investigate this situation and determine who is behind it."

Most interesting, I thought, and a polite way of issuing what seemed to be a royal decree.

"I appreciate your confidence, sir," Brodie replied.

"You hesitate?"

"Such matters are often withheld for reasons that would make it impossible to provide assistance."

A thoughtful and accurate response for something we had encountered in the past.

Those of the upper classes prioritized their good names and titles at all costs. There were a few like my great aunt who didn't give a fig about such posturing and overblown ideas or self-importance.

Yet, by and large, it was true of mainstream society, and most particularly the royal family. They had the reputation of "closing ranks" as it were in order to protect one of their own, no matter the situation, whether it was the latest mischief or scandal that might reflect badly.

Case in point, Prince Albert's many affairs, a mistress or two, and other transgressions that no one knew about because of aforementioned habit of protecting their own at all costs. It did make the prospect of investigating the matter of young Lord Salisbery's death very near impossible.

"Very well." His Highness abruptly turned to me.

"You will excuse us, Lady Forsythe."

It was not a request.

"Ye are aware of her efforts on yer behalf in the past," Brodie reminded him before I could respond. "Anything ye discuss with me, ye may discuss with the both of us."

It was obviously not what Prince Albert expected given the surprised expression on his face.

"I am well aware, Mr. Brodie, and I meant no offense."

This was added with a look over at myself.

"There is another matter," Brodie added.

I did notice that the accent from his youth on the streets of Edinburgh seemed to thicken when he was angered over something. Not that it had ever been directed at me. Ha!

"If we are to consider yer request," he continued. "It would be with yer word that we are to have full authority and control of the case with no interference."

"If I do not agree?" Prince Albert challenged.

"Then we will bid ye good day, sir."

The atmosphere in the room was so thick one could have cut it with a knife.

"I am reminded that the Scots can be particularly stubborn."

I would have laughed if the situation wasn't so serious.

"I make no apologies, sir," Brodie told him. He stood to leave.

"Very well," HRH replied somewhat sharply. "You have full control of the investigation into the matter, but I would ask for discretion at all times."

Brodie nodded. It was obvious he had hoped his demand would be the end of the matter. And now...

"We will need to meet with Lord Salisbery for details of that evening."

Prince Albert nodded. "I will inform him." He turned to me.

"I believe you are acquainted with him?"

Only socially and briefly at that. Yet, I nodded. There was someone who might be able to assist with that—my great aunt.

"Who else knows about this note," Brodie pointed to the envelope that he had set aside on the table.

"Only Lord Salisbery, my secretary Sir Knollys, and myself. Sir Knollys received it at Marlborough House with a note from Lord Salisbery. He opens all my personal correspondence."

"What of the driver from that night? Has he been questioned?"

"Lord Salisbery has not received word of that from the Metropolitan Police."

"Is Lord Salisbery presently in London?"

"He is. This matter is most important to him."

"Then I would suggest ye send word to him that we need to meet in order to make our usual inquiries, and we will require the full cooperation of the MET."

"Then we are agreed in the matter?" HRH inquired.

"We will make our usual inquiries as soon as we have met with Lord Salisbery. The sooner the better, of course."

"We are hosting a party, Wednesday this week, a birthday celebration. It would be the perfect opportunity for you to meet with Lord Salisbery." HRH looked at me then.

"I will see that you receive invitations."

I could almost hear Brodie groan. He attended formal celebrations under duress.

That was in two days' time. It would provide time for me to make inquiries with the stationer I used regarding the note found on young Lord Salisbery.

It would also provide Brodie with time to learn what the police knew about the case through those he had worked with in the past.

Three

"WHAT ARE YOU THINKING," I inquired as we made the ride this morning across London to the office on The Strand.

Brodie sat across from me in the coach, elbow braced on the window's edge, chin propped on his hand as he stared out the opening with a thoughtful frown. That dark gaze met mine.

He had said little about our meeting with HRH the previous evening, but I knew he was turning it over in his mind, considering the merits of it...considering the difficulties that would be involved. It had been there this morning over breakfast as well.

"I'm thinkin' that matters involving the nobility are more often than not complicated and difficult, as ye well know. They have that penchant for secrecy in order to protect their good name. And dinna look at me with yer brow raised like that, Mikaela Forsythe. Ye know well my meanin', and truth is that ye and perhaps her Ladyship are the rare exceptions."

It was not the first time the difference between our classes had raised its head. I usually chose to ignore it. It made no difference to me.

"Most will do anything to protect their good name, title, and reputation, and it can make a case impossible to solve, not to mention dangerous."

He was right, of course. We had both encountered that difficulty in past inquiries. While I understood where it came from, I refused to accept it when lives were at stake.

"We should at least meet with Lord Salisbery," I pointed out. "And then decide if there is any way that we may help in the matter. If not, we will simply have to be honest with both Lord Salisbery and His Highness."

The look he gave me indicated that he didn't think it would be that simple. Yet, he said nothing more.

Mr. Cavendish met us on the sidewalk as we arrived.

Brodie paid the driver, then inquired about the work that was being done to the building.

"There was a bit of difficulty yesterday," Mr. Cavendish replied. "The workmen arrived to finish the lift and connect the electric..."

"And the difficulty?" I inquired.

"The hound managed to get himself trapped in the bloody thing between the first and second floor. The workmen had to disconnect the electric, then lower the compartment by hand crank.

"They said that never happened before, as if the lever inside the compartment might have been meddled with. Although I cannot imagine how it might have happened. It's all good now."

Most interesting, I thought. Particularly since it seemed that there was no food or a body part involved. Rupert had survived the ordeal and was already out and about on the streets.

"I will take the stairs," Brodie announced as I went to inspect the compartment that contained the lift with a door that opened near the alcove.

I stepped inside the compartment, closed the gate, then engaged the lever. There was a faint humming sound as the compartment slowly lifted, then arrived at the second-floor landing and stopped with a soft bump. I opened the gate and stepped out onto the landing.

"Marvelous," I announced as Brodie stood waiting at the door to the office. "Particularly when the weather sets in, no need for a mad dash up the stairs in the rain. And it does increase the value of the building."

He was not convinced. "And cost a bloody fortune."

I ignored that. The cost had actually been quite reasonable, when figured in with the other improvements that were being made. And, as I had previously pointed out to him, once the work was completed, the rents for the other parts of the building would more than cover any cost for the lift.

"Most of the professional buildings about London have them now," I reminded him. "I have heard that someone is working on an inclined elevator to take passengers from one point to another," I continued as I joined him at the door to the office.

"Much like climbing a hill, but the machine does it instead with individual steps that move along."

"I suppose ye will be wanting one installed here," he commented.

"It might present a difficulty for Mr. Cavendish." I smothered a smile as I replied. "It has been described as a series of steps that move by way of a belt."

He shook his head. "I prefer things that dinna move under my feet."

"We are very near the new century, Mr. Brodie," I pointed out. "There is talk that the underground tube across the whole of London will be opened very soon."

"Stairs that move, a train that moves through an underground tube," he replied as he opened the door to the office and waited for me to enter before him. "The next thing ye know, people will be flying about in contraptions with wings. I would not put it past her ladyship to acquire one."

He did have a point there.

"Far more efficient than an air ship," I pointed out, reminding him of that prior adventure over the streets of London.

"Those things appeal to ye, do they?"

"Along with some old-fashioned things," I replied, as the *old-fashioned* man crossed the office and set coal in the stove.

While he prodded the fire back to life, I went to the chalkboard and added the notes I'd made in my notebook from our meeting the previous afternoon with His Royal Highness.

Before we left Mayfair, Brodie had made contact with Mr. Dooley, an Inspector with the MET, and an old friend from their days working together. He had agreed to meet with Brodie late in the morning at a coffee shop a distance from the stationhouse where Mr. Dooley was assigned, in order to avoid being seen by any of the constables or others who might raise questions about their meeting.

Most particularly Mr. Abberline, who had recently been reinstated as Chief Inspector after being suspended for a period of time over his misconduct in one of our previous cases.

Needless to say, there were still difficult feelings over the situation on the part of both parties. Personally, I would have preferred to see the man permanently removed from the police service. He was quite unscrupulous, driven by his own ambitions. In short, a thoroughly disgusting man. And he was quite short in stature.

I had my own opinion in that regard. In my experience, it did seem as though men lacking in height were determined to make up for that shortcoming by other means. It did appear to be about power, or lack thereof.

I thought of what I had read about Napoleon Bonaparte, quite short it seems from written accounts. I was most appreciative that Brodie was tall. He was self-assured with no penchant for exercising his authority over another. Unless provoked, of course. But that came from his early life on the streets and some sort of survival instinct.

"What is that look for?" he inquired now as he prepared for his meeting with Inspector Dooley.

He was not in the habit of wearing a tie. However, I had persuaded him that it had a way of setting him apart under certain circumstances.

This morning, he had added one, tying it as if he would rather have avoided the whole thing—which of course he did.

I had finished my notes and went to assist.

"I am most grateful that you are quite tall," I commented as I straightened his tie for him.

His eyes narrowed in speculation. He was most definitely not accustomed to receiving compliments.

"What might that have to do with matters?"

I finished tying.

"I have never fancied short men. They do seem to constantly be making up for that inadequacy."

"Inadequacy? Would that include the Greek guide I found ye with some years before in yer misguided youth?"

"Misguided?" I inquired as he pulled me against him.

"Aye, taking yerself off with a man ye didna know could have been dangerous."

Though it had been several years earlier, it was obvious that he had not dismissed it.

"Being abducted by yourself could have been dangerous," I pointed out. "You might have had your way with me."

He shook his head. "I did not abduct ye. And I was not in the habit of taking advantage of young women full of themselves. The fact was that I was being paid a great deal to bring ye safely back to London by her ladyship."

"How mercenary of you, Mr. Brodie."

"Ah, well, the rent was due for the office, and I had just finished another case at the time."

It was so like him to dismiss it as nothing more than another case or well-paid errand.

"There was that other part though."

Other part?

"What was that?" I demanded with some pique at being reduced to an errand.

"Ye are a troublesome baggage. Strong-willed, and there was that part on the boat when ye threatened to pitch me overboard into the sea. I was tempted to bind ye and tie a cloth over yer mouth. Ye do have a way with words. It's that temper of yers."

How very endearing, I thought. "You seem to have survived."

That dark gaze met mine. "I prefer a challenge. I'd never met a lady who knew those words."

Yes, well...I had tried to temper my vocabulary since. I had discovered other effective means.

He kissed me quite thoroughly, which made me consider that we might perhaps put off our inquiries for the day?

His hands slipped onto my shoulders then he gently set me from him.

"I will see ye at the townhouse," he said in parting.

I knew that he also intended to visit the scene of the crime, as he called it, with that former police inspector's perspective.

"Perhaps," I replied.

He could be such a devil, and it was all that I could think of in the moment. And then there was that smile curving one corner of his mouth.

"Then we can discuss what we learned."

As I said, such a devil. He knew perfectly well that I would want to know everything he was able to learn about the police investigation into young Lord Salisbery's murder, as well as his thoughts about where it had taken place.

After he left, I seized my travel bag with my notebook and left the office as well.

While he met with Mr. Dooley, I intended to call on the print shop that had provided calling cards for our inquiry business.

I was hoping to learn what the owner of the shop might be able to tell me about the stationary used for the note that was found with young Lord Salisbery the night of the robbery and murder.

As we set off, I took the lift down from the second floor to the street as Brodie took the stairs once again.

"It is quite marvelous," I told him again when he arrived on the landing near the alcove. "And it saves time." That was something that should appeal to him.

"As long as the hound stays out of the bloody thing."

"Yes, I know. And you prefer things that don't move under

your feet," I replied as I stepped past him and gave the driver Mr. Cavendish had summoned the destination of the print shop on Fleet Street.

"Do be careful," I told him as I stepped up into coach. "Coaches can be most dangerous...they move under your feet."

There was undoubtedly a comment about that, but I failed to hear it as we set off.

The ride to Fleet Street was not long, and I arrived just after ten o'clock in the morning.

In addition to calling cards, they also provided notebooks and stationery, and were under contract with my publisher to print my books.

The clerk at the counter greeted me cordially, "Good morning, Lady Forsythe. How may I assist you this morning? More calling cards?"

"I would like to speak with Mr. Marsden regarding another matter if he is available," I explained.

The clerk let him know, and he appeared from the back of his shop.

"Good morning, Lady Forsythe."

I explained that I needed his assistance in identifying a certain piece of paper and where it might have been purchased.

"Ah, part of your next inquiry case, perhaps?" he commented.

"If we might meet privately," I suggested.

It was my intention to keep the note and that message private for now. That required having him examine the envelope it had been left in, which was stained with blood.

He nodded. "Of course." And directed me toward his office.

He closed the door for privacy as I took the envelope out of my bag. I laid the envelope on his desk.

"I'm hoping you might be able to tell me something about this."

I didn't mention that the paper was quite different from any I had used in the past, my great aunt's formal stationary with the family crest, nor other paper I was familiar with—found in the dailies, or the paper in my books.

He picked up the envelope to inspect it, and I caught the change in his expression when he saw the stain across the front of it.

He gently stroked the unmarred flap, then held the envelope up to the overhead light.

"Just as I thought." He very carefully laid it back on the desk. "The paper the envelope was made from is handmade, a very old, time-consuming process, and quite expensive. I have not had a request for it in some time. It is called rag paper, quite different from paper used for newspapers and books, or quality white paper for correspondence, or the usual notepaper requested for writing letters."

"Who might use this?" I inquired.

"As I said, it is quite expensive. Those who could afford it, of course, the upper classes, perhaps the Queen," he suggested, then had a thoughtful expression. "I might have a sample of this in one of my folders. If you have the time...?"

"Yes, of course."

He went to the cabinet behind his desk and pulled down a thick leather-bound folder. He opened it atop the desk.

"I keep all samples of paper that I've used over the years, and a file for customers that lists the paper they've used in the past for their print orders, as you well know."

There were several samples. He found the one he was looking for and held it up.

"This is a sample of rag paper before it's printed with

anything." He handed the sample to me. It was thick and I could feel raised areas that had been woven into the paper.

"Those are cotton fibers, very similar to the material in the envelope. It requires a very careful printing process. It is also very durable, where other types of paper might yellow or become quite brittle and crumble over time."

"Are there those who specialize in using rag paper, who might be able to tell me who placed an order for this envelope?"

"The older gentleman, Hiram Bridgeforth, whom I apprenticed with, kept a stock of it, but that was quite a long time ago. Most printers use thick wood pulp paper for stationery, announcements, and calling cards, with notepaper such as the ones I bind for diaries, journals, notebooks and your novels.

"I apologize that I cannot tell you more, Lady Forsythe?" He handed the envelope back to me.

I nodded and thanked him for his time and information. Before leaving, I purchased two of his notebooks.

"I look forward to your next novel. Mr. Warren has said that it will be forthcoming for print."

My latest Emma novel was regarding a case that had taken Brodie and I to France and then Budapest. I had finished it a few months earlier and delivered it to my publisher, who was now my sister's husband.

It was still early in the day as I left the stationer's shop, that envelope and note tucked into my current notebook. I had learned something potentially important in my visit with Mr. Marsden, but I had no idea what it might mean—expensive, somewhat rare stationery that few people used any more. Except perhaps for someone of the upper class?

It was some time yet until I was to meet Brodie back at the

townhouse in Mayfair, and I directed the driver to Sussex Square.

Lily, quite a young woman now, had been in somewhat of a somber mood at the birthday celebration for my great aunt.

"The usual sort of thing," my sister had commented at the time. "You must remember it from our own time before leaving for France where we wouldn't see most of our friends here in London except on holiday."

It was a reminder of my part in bringing Lily to London as my ward, and I decided to take the opportunity to call on them.

Four

BRODIE

THE JAMPOT COFFEEHOUSE, as it was referred to, so-called because it was founded when Jamaican coffee was first brought to London, was just off Cornhill at the edge of the financial district. It was an unlikely place to encounter any of the lads from the MET or Chief Inspector Abberline.

Inspector Dooley was there when he arrived and nodded a greeting from a table near the rear of the establishment where either one might make a quick departure if needed.

He had contacted Dooley the previous afternoon in an effort to learn what progress the MET had made with the robbery and murder of young Lord Salisbery.

Dooley had provided valuable information in the past for their inquiry cases, under the table so to speak, when Brodie's direct inquiries at the MET had met with:

Obstacles. "We're not allowed to give out that information, Mr. Brodie."

Delays. "I put in the request, sir, but there's been no response from high up as yet."

Or no response at all.

As if the information had simply disappeared into the London fog, when time was most important, and other lives might very well have been in danger.

More often than not the information was important, and they had both avoided any confrontation with those "higher up" in the matter with a common excuse that the information was learned from "another source" that remained nameless when questioned.

To his way of thinking, the most important thing was solving the crime. If it required bending the rules from time to time, or acquiring information that might not otherwise be available, he was not one to lose sleep over the matter.

He took the chair opposite Dooley that faced out to the entrance if anyone from the service should arrive at the coffee-house. He was not of a mind to put his friend in a difficult situation.

Mr. Dooley waved down the man behind the counter to bring another cup of coffee.

"The case you inquired about has been difficult," Dooley commented, the accent of years in the Irish countryside still there after over twenty years in London.

"Robbery?" Brodie asked as the coffee warmed his belly.

"That would seem to be the motive. The young man apparently resisted..."

And robbery, frequent on the streets of London, particularly late at night, became murder.

"What about the club attendant?"

"He was questioned. A driver arrived as usual when the call

was put out. The attendant saw the young man to the coach, as usual. Then they were on their way."

"Private coach?" Brodie asked.

Dooley shook his head. "One of the city services. It seems the young man wanted to avoid any scrutiny and usually had a driver called for."

Brodie sat back in his chair, turning over the information.

"Did the attendant notice anything unusual in Salisbery's manner?"

"Only that he was well into his cups when he left."

"What time was that?"

"Near three in the morning. He'd been gaming most of the night, and...other activities."

"A woman?"

Dooley nodded. "The usual 'menu' according to the attendant. He said she goes by the name of Lady Dumont."

Lady Dumont. It was not the first time that such a woman would stylize herself as a 'lady', except the *lady* he was married too. Titles had a way of increasing the appeal, the clientele, not to mention the compensation.

"However," Dooley continued, "we have not been able to question her in the matter. She seems to have disappeared, perhaps due to the events of the evening and a reluctance to be questioned by the police."

"Where does the *lady* live?"

"Lady Dumont?" I commented as Brodie recounted his meeting with Mr. Dooley.

I sat across from him, my boots on the floor, my stockinged feet propped across his knee as we shared what we each learned with our inquiries. He was presently rubbing my right foot after my adventures with Lily at Sussex Square.

Upon my arrival, she had immediately challenged me to a duel with weapons from the Sword Room. It contained an impressive collection of rapiers, swords, shields, and a claymore or two, not to mention other assorted daggers, pikes, and several flint lock pistols and other weapons acquired by generations of Montgomerys.

In the interest of preserving the room, we had taken the challenge out onto the green. Needless to say, I was not appropriately dressed for the challenge, with a long skirt and inappropriate footwear.

But who might be when unexpectedly attacked, I rationalized, as I carried on with the duel, much to the complaint of my feet afterward. My consolation was that I had won the challenge.

"Do ye know the woman?" Brodie asked with a doubtful expression.

Admittedly, I did not usually associate with enterprising "ladies of the night," other than a previous case. However...

"Most inventive," I replied.

"Her name or her profession?" he asked with a sip of Old Lodge whisky.

Cheeky fellow. I would have commented on that, except I did not want to interrupt his attention which was now on my left foot.

"Lady Dumont is a character in a somewhat risqué novel that was written several years ago."

"A novel?"

"Not the sort that I write. I prefer murder."

"I'll have to remember that," he replied as he gently

massaged my toes that had suffered somewhat from the afternoon duel.

"She was a notorious character who contributed to the demise of Lord Wimberley, another character in the novel. It was quite difficult to obtain a copy since it was banned for a while."

"Ye prevailed of course."

"A friend managed to acquire it and passed it to me."

"A friend?"

Not that he believed it for a moment.

"And just how did the man meet his end?"

I gave him a very long look with a smile. He did have the reputation for being quite clever at figuring things out.

"I'll have to remember that as well." He reached across and took my glass from me.

"No more for ye, if I'm to live through the night."

I laughed, yet there was another matter that I had learned of that afternoon.

"Lily mentioned that she spoke to you about returning to Edinburgh the other evening, rather than leaving for Paris after the new year."

She had spoken of it to me but hadn't shared what his response was. I was aware that she looked to him as a sort of father figure, with their similar backgrounds and experience in Edinburgh.

"She does seem to value your thoughts on important matters. What did you tell her?"

He proceeded to massage my toes. "That it was not for me to say," he replied. "I am not a good example."

"You and Munro are perfect examples. You've come from the same place and some of the same circumstances," I pointed out. "And there have been times when she and I have had those sorts of discussions, and she looks at me as if..."

"As if, what?" he replied.

"She reminds me too much of me, headstrong, fearless at times, and..."

"Stubborn?" he suggested as he looked up.

"Perhaps a little," I conceded. "Yet you have such a marvelous way of knowing people, 'reading' them as you call it, and she does trust you."

I had experienced that first hand myself, admittedly a bit disconcerting at times when I had learned early on to keep my thoughts to myself and then carry on as a sort of self-preservation as my great aunt called it. He had changed that.

"What advice did you give her?" I then asked.

"I told her that my experience was not the example to follow. I also explained that an education, such as ye have, will take her far as she is intelligent, and it would provide her opportunities that she wouldn't have otherwise."

"It appears that you weren't entirely able to dissuade her," I concluded.

He looked at me with that dark gaze. I could have sworn there was amusement there.

"As I have been able to dissuade ye from doing something that ye shouldna do?"

"I have no idea what you are speaking of."

He proceeded to tickle the bottom of my foot, and my toes curled. The only thing that prevented further assault of my foot was the service bell that rang on the landing followed by...a knock at the door.

Brodie cursed, then went to the door and yanked it open. Mr. Cavendish grinned up at him.

"An envelope arrived with one of those gold seals on it. I

thought it might be important and brought it up straight away."

I smothered a smile as I set order to my skirts and crossed the office in my stockinged feet. He had obviously used the lift.

"Excellent, thank you," I complimented Mr. Cavendish. "Most efficient."

He tipped his cap. "I knew you would want it in short order."

He spun around on his platform and returned down the companionway toward the newly installed lift.

"Aye, efficient," Brodie commented.

He handed me the embossed envelope that had been delivered from Marlborough House.

I opened it. "An official invitation, it seems, from the Prince of Wales for his birthday celebration tomorrow evening," I announced.

Five

MARLBOROUGH HOUSE

THE ROYAL MANOR was located at The Mall, near St. James's Park in Westminster, set amidst a park with a stone wall along the roadway that enclosed the grounds and the manor.

The tree-lined roadway along The Mall passed several stately buildings at the edge of St. James's Park that included private men's clubs, stately residences, along with upper class shopping. and the War Office.

In the faint light from the lantern inside the coach, I caught Brodie's expression. It could be more accurately described as distracted. In that way he had of turning over what we had learned in his thoughts, little as it was. Our driver pulled through the gated entrance, then pulled to a stop where Brodie presented our engraved invitation.

The guard handed the invitation back and nodded to our driver, then we continued to the cobbled courtyard flanked on either side by a four-story wing of the mansion. Those wings contained private rooms, sitting rooms, and other private chambers of the 'Marlborough Lot' as they were called, which included gaming rooms, as well as the Prince of Wales's office, those of advisers, and an enormous library that I had found to be most interesting on a past visit.

"Good God!" Brodie remarked at the lights that glowed on all floors of the mansion. "How many rooms does a man need to lay his head?"

This from a man who was raised on the streets as a child and had lain his head wherever it was safe for a few hours or had not when it wasn't.

"Several, I would guess, with his assortment of mistresses and other casual acquaintances," I replied, with no need to elaborate further.

"Have ye been here before?"

"I attended a holiday celebration some years ago with my sister and Aunt Antonia. It was all quite boring, and I persuaded Linnie to go exploring," I added.

"It was quite an adventure. We interrupted a well-known lady *in flagrante* with a man who was not her husband. Most entertaining and revealing regarding the '*act*' between a man and woman."

"Why am I not surprised?"

Our driver stopped at the entryway to the main entrance hall, and we stepped down from the coach. Two liveried attendants flanked the entrance, and Brodie once more presented our invitation. We then made our way, along with other guests, into the main hall.

It was ornately decorated with bunting and swags that led into the grand saloon.

I felt Brodie's hand on my arm as we joined the procession of well-wishers who had been invited to join the celebration and now offered their best wishes and greetings to HRH and the Princess of Wales. Along with Prince George and his wife,

Mary of Teck, recently married in July, and sister Princess Louise, Duchess of Fife and her husband.

"Lady Forsythe," HRH greeted me with a keen eye then to Brodie. "We are pleased that you have joined us this evening, and Mr. Brodie. It is good to see you as well. Perhaps the evening will allow the opportunity for us to speak of your work."

I caught the unspoken comment beneath the formality.

"Of course," Brodie replied.

"Lady Montgomery arrived earlier," the Princess of Wales then informed us. "Always a pleasure to see her once more. She does make the festivities quite lively."

With that, we moved ahead toward the saloon. I took the opportunity to point out guests I knew.

"Lord Salisbery?" Brodie inquired.

With a look about, I finally saw him. "Near the arched entrance to the great hall, speaking with a man wearing an obvious wig and wine-colored waistcoat."

He watched both men.

"And the man who just approached them?"

"Sir Knollys, His Highness's personal secretary."

It did appear that the Prince of Wales wasted no time as Sir Knollys glanced toward us and then approached.

"Mr. Brodie, His Highness has asked if you might join him and Lord Salisbery in the library."

Brodie gave me a look, then replied, "Of course."

He was no stranger to royal encounters and HRH had spoken of a meeting that would be easily accommodated at the gathering. Still, there was some urgency in Sir Knollys's manner.

And it very much appeared that I was not to be included. I ignored the omission as it was not the first time. But far more important, I had no desire to cause a scene or to delay his meeting with Lord Salisbery.

It was one of those things that was most irritating—putting a woman in her place. Said place being the receiving line at a society function or the bedroom.

Not my first experience, and assuredly not the last. However, I knew that Brodie would share everything with me afterward, and it was possible that Lord Salisbery would reveal things with him that he would not otherwise in my presence.

I smiled at Sir Knollys as they departed for the library. He was, after all, simply performing his duties. Yet I was mindful to keep any comment to myself.

I watched as they departed, then went in search of my great aunt. Finding her in the crowded saloon was not difficult. She looked up as I approached.

"Here you are!" she greeted me as she sailed toward me in a brilliant blue gown that emphasized her silver hair and vivid blue eyes.

She did have a way of parting the crowds with a simple nod and a smile as she greeted one guest, then another.

"So good to see you again, Arthur."

"Jonathan, how marvelous and your lovely lady as well," she greeted them as she swept toward me. It was quite entertaining to watch her.

The last greeting was for Lady Sharp, who had taken her husband's name and whose features were quite...sharp! To the point of being almost frightening. Proof that title and wealth could always be relied upon to acquire a husband.

"Mikaela, dear." She finally reached me and pressed a kiss to my cheek. "So good to see you again." She looked about as if searching for someone.

"And Brodie?" she inquired. "Or was there some matter

that required his attention elsewhere?" She leaned in close. "I did see him with Sir Knollys and Lord Salisbery. So very tragic about his son."

Her subtle way of asking about our new inquiry case. Sly like a fox.

"Will the Queen be attending?" I inquired as a diversion for the conversation.

She gave me a knowing look but chose not to pursue the question.

"It is doubtful," she replied instead. "She chooses to avoid such things, still in mourning after all these years. Such a waste, and there is the estrangement between her and the Prince of Wales. It might prove difficult with the Marlborough Set here for the festivities, considering the usual rumors of their activities here.

"Hunting parties, they call them. The question might be just what or whom is the quarry."

Aunt Antonia, who had experienced several decades of royal scandals and rumored liaisons, was always most entertaining. She was not usually concerned about proprieties over such things, which admittedly had included her own ancestors.

"Do you think that perhaps she embellishes her stories?" my sister had once asked after a particularly colorful story that our great aunt had shared.

I sincerely doubted it. She was merely honest in that way of someone who had experienced such things and dared anyone to contradict her.

"Ah, Sir Richard Braithwaite has arrived," Aunt Antonia exclaimed now with a nod across the room. "A schoolmate of the Prince of Wales. From their university days. There were four of them—reckless, carrying on as young men have a way of doing, getting themselves into, shall we call them 'situations,' the way young men have a habit of doing when they believe themselves invincible and above the law.

"There was more than one scandal that made the newspapers, and the one where Prince Albert was forced to intervene on the Prince of Wales's behalf. The poor man died shortly after, and it is said the Queen blamed young Albert for the 'difficulty of the situation' and has never forgiven him."

She nodded a greeting to Sir Braithwaite, and he in turn nodded across the floor of the saloon with its sweeping staircases, paintings of royal ancestors that filled the walls in gilt frames, and full-sized statues looking down on the festivities.

"The newspapers called them the Four Horsemen of the Apocalypse in one article before it was banned from referring to them as such," she continued with that smile. "However, they did seem to revel in the attention, until the Queen stepped in and ended it all.

"They have all been part of the Marlborough Set since, as well as occupying high level positions."

Most interesting, I thought, as we continued around the enormous room and I did wonder what those statues set upon the walls high above the room and at the balustrade of the landing to the second floor might have witnessed of the Prince of Wales's indiscretions in the past.

"I see that they have brought out champagne for the guests, a favorite of the Princess of Wales," Aunt Antonia commented. "I suppose that will have to do. I have always thought it to be highly overrated."

A comment from a *connoisseur* with a preference for her own Old Lodge whisky.

"You're finally here!"

That excited exclamation rushed toward us in a wave of

dark emerald-green that emphasized the young woman's dark eyes and dark hair that lay over one shoulder.

I was taken somewhat by surprise as I was familiar with Lily in a walking skirt and blouse for lessons with her tutor, or a dueling costume when practicing in the sword room.

I was reminded of Brodie's comment that she was no longer the young girl we had brought from Edinburgh after one of our inquiry cases, but a young woman. And a beautiful young woman, according to the stares that followed her.

Not that she was aware as she joined us.

"Bloody hell, this gown is tight. I can hardly breathe." The Scots accent was there, subtle, but still there along with her blunt assessment of the gown.

"However, do ye wear such clothes? And a bloody corset!" she added.

"I chose to escape as many society parties as possible," I confessed, thoroughly enjoying her comment that included rolling those dark eyes.

Of course, the tightness of the gown might have something to do with the way it fits now. She had worn it some months before, as I remembered. However, she had still seemed quite the young girl then. No longer, it seemed, as Brodie had reminded me.

"And the young men," she continued. "I had to threaten to take one of them down if he touched me again. As if he thought he could."

Those eyes narrowed. "He laughed."

Foolish on the part of the young man. It was undoubtedly best that the temptation was removed, for now. I hooked my arm through hers. "Let's escape," I suggested. "There is an impressive trophy room on the second floor that I explored in the past."

A temporary reprieve at best from any further questions regarding Brodie from my great aunt, but one, nevertheless.

Several other guests had escaped the saloon and gathered in small groups in the hallway on the second floor and in the various rooms that were not otherwise private rooms.

That included the library, the portrait room with historic portraits that went back two hundred years—not as impressive as those at Sussex Square, according to Lily, and the trophy room with walls lined with the heads of red deer, wild boar, and stuffed partridge and pheasant adorning the walls as if in flight.

Deer and boar looked down on us, as well as several other guests.

"For sport?" Lily commented hardly impressed. "How many people would those animals feed?"

Not unlike Brodie's comment about the size of Marlborough House.

I understood her feelings, having been raised in a whorehouse in her early years. And before that? On the streets of Edinburgh, her family unknown, where food might have been a luxury.

I had to agree that it was excessive. And merely for sport?

"I agree with you, young woman. Quite ghastly." A comment with a slight accent.

"Lady Forsythe, you must introduce me to this enlightened young woman."

I turned and recognized Lady Blanche Somerset, Baroness Waterford.

I had met the Baroness previously. She was not beautiful but quite striking in that way of those who know their worth, and everyone else could take a flying leap.

While we had encountered each other just after my last year

in Paris and that unique experience in Greece, I remembered her from a reception at Sussex Square.

"I have heard interesting rumors about your recent exploits, Lady Forsythe. Is this young lady a member of the family or perhaps a protégée?"

Lily maintained that curious yet cautious demeanor that had not changed since she first arrived in London as I made introductions.

"My ward, Lily Montgomery."

"Ah, a member of that illustrious family. I thought I saw Lady Antonia earlier. You are part of a remarkable family," she continued. "Quite colorful, but we all have our infamous ghosts. Wouldn't you agree, Lady Forsythe?"

I did agree. Most of ours were well documented, aside from a highwayman or two and a well-known pirate for which there were only rumors and old stories.

"And quite insightful, my dear," Lady Blanche told Lily. "I have never understood the fascination with killing a helpless animal."

She stared at the boar. "Perhaps not completely helpless. One can only hope that the creature gave as good as it got."

A unique perspective that I had not previously encountered among my great aunt's circle of friends. I could tell that Lily was quite impressed.

"Have you ever hunted, your ladyship?" she inquired.

"Only men, my dear," she replied with candor and a wink over at me. "That is something that requires great skill. For the most part, a great many men are not worth the effort.

"Now, you must tell me where you acquired that enlightened attitude, and we shall no doubt offend several others here, if Lady Forsythe does not mind."

I caught Lily's glance. She was enjoying herself very much. She had found another kindred spirit.

"Not at all. I have seen it before. I will see you back downstairs when you finish your tour," I told her.

I did want very much to see if Brodie had returned from his meeting with the Prince of Wales and Lord Salisbery. And I was confident that Lily was in good company.

~

LILY

The room and the displays were impressive, if one didn't mind being surrounded by dead animals.

I thought it was sad as I continued about the room with Baroness Waterford.

"It's about the hunt," she explained. "There is something quite primitive in most men—the need to hunt, chase some poor creature down, and then kill it. Then what do you have? Heads on a wall."

We continued about the room as other guests came into the large room and others left to return to the saloon below.

"I have never been one to be put in my place." She gave me a long look, and a smile. "I sense you are not either. Oh, do look at this creature, a lion. No doubt from foreign travels. He looks as if he might leap through the wall. A magnificent creature."

"We saw several when Lady Antonia and I traveled to Africa," I replied. "They are beautiful. We didn't hunt them," I assured her.

"A woman after my own heart," Lady Blanche replied.

I liked her very much—for a titled lady. She wasn't afraid to speak her mind and didn't give airs like some.

She reminded me of Lady Antonia and Mikaela, sure of herself, bold, and not at all concerned about what anyone thought or overheard, even as I saw more than one head turn at a comment she made.

"Let us explore the next room," she suggested.

As we left the trophy room, there was a startling sound very near and shouts of alarm, then curses.

"Good heavens, what is this about?" the Baroness said as I turned and saw two men struggling only a few feet away.

One, quite young, fought his attacker, but he was thrown back across the railing. I watched, horrified as the young man was then thrown over the railing to startled screams from the floor below.

A blow caught me on the shoulder as his attacker ran past. His gaze briefly met mine, then I was roughly shoved aside.

The hallway that led to stairway was in chaos as another woman screamed and guests fled the corridor and down the stairs.

"That poor young man...!" Someone else exclaimed, as a woman who stood nearby suddenly collapsed in a faint.

I ran to the railing. The young man lay sprawled at the floor below, staring up at everyone who gathered round as a pool of blood spread beneath his head.

Shouts went out for the royal guards as someone else called out for a physician, the birthday celebration turning into a horrifying scene.

"Did you see it?" a gentleman nearby asked another. "There was a struggle... He pushed that poor young man over the railing..." Another exclaimed, "Young Anthony, the son of Sir Huntingdon," as royal guards rushed into the saloon below.

And from another, "Did you see the man?"

"He fled toward the end of the hallway. That door…"

As everyone stood about blathering and a young man lay at the floor below, the culprit was escaping!

Baroness Waterford called after me as I gathered up my skirts and ran toward the end of the hallway and that door.

It opened onto the stairway that led down to the main floor below, not unlike the one at Sussex Square and no doubt to the kitchen, and the servants' quarters.

I heard a door snap closed below and followed that sound down the stairs lit by overhead electric.

The door at the bottom of the stairs opened onto a hallway near the kitchens, where I encountered two servants with an enormous cake on a rolling cart, unaware of what had just happened.

"A man came this way…"

They stared at me in confusion.

"Did ye see him?" I demanded.

One of the servants pointed to a back entrance.

Who expected such a situation in such a well-guarded place. I grabbed the silver cake knife from the tray, then ran out through that entrance and onto the green.

Light from the windows of the mansion and torches along the driveway to the stables lit up the green, and I caught sight of a shadowy figure that fled there. He reached the edge of the green, then disappeared among the private coaches and broughams that lined the parkway.

I ran after him, across the green, then across the parkway and cursed. He could be hiding anywhere among the coaches, drivers, and horse teams. Or he might have already reached the throughfare beyond that stone wall.

A hand closed around my upper arm and spun me around.

I brought the knife up at the same time I swept the feet out from under my attacker the way Mikaela had taught me.

My attacker hit the ground with a string of curses in the Scots, and a sharp blue gaze met mine in the light from a nearby lantern.

"Wot the devil?" he snapped.

I stared down at Munro, sprawled at my feet. "A man ran this way. Did ye see him?"

Six

"WHAT DID YE SEE?" Brodie asked Lily, as we gathered in the first-floor library at Marlborough House.

It was well past midnight, and needless to say, the birthday celebration for the Prince of Wales had taken a deadly turn.

Most of the guests had departed, their drivers crowding the courtyard at the main entrance as word reached them.

A physician had been summoned, but there was nothing to be done for the poor young man who had tragically fallen over the balustrade of the stairway from the second floor. A "dreadful accident" the guests whispered among themselves as they departed.

A police van had arrived and taken the young man's body to a private mortuary. The Prince of Wales stood with a hand on the shoulder of his old friend, Sir Huntingdon, who sat at a table, his head hung in disbelief; Lady Huntingdon in the private drawing room, currently being attended by the physician.

"I don't understand." Sir Huntingdon looked up at the man he'd known since their university days who would one day be king. The barriers had been dropped with the horrific event of the evening.

Brodie and I had been asked to join the Prince of Wales and Sir Huntingdon in the library, along with Lily and Munro. I looked over at Lily. She sat quietly at a side table in the library with Munro nearby.

She had shown amazing composure when Munro had escorted her back to Marlborough House after that encounter near the stables.

In the chaos and horror among the guests, it did seem that she was the one person who had gotten a good look at the man who assaulted young Huntingdon.

"An accident?" Sir Huntingdon exclaimed, incredulous, his voice breaking. "How could this happen?"

He shook his head, his hand resting on the note with that chilling message that was found inside his son's coat:

And then there was one...

"Young Salisbery, and now this? What does it mean?" he asked with the grief of a father who has just lost a son, still unable to comprehend what had happened.

I saw the look that passed between Brodie and the Prince of Wales.

"There are matters to be discussed," his Highness replied with the familiarity of a long-time friend.

"However, not tonight," he added. "You must see to your wife. Take her home. We will speak of this tomorrow."

Not precisely an order to be obeyed, but most definitely not a conversation they would have now. Prince Edward nodded to Sir Knollys.

"You will please escort Sir Huntingdon so that he may join

Lady Huntingdon, and you will inform the Royal Guard that they are needed immediately."

In that way that Sir Knollys had served the Prince of Wales for some time, it was obvious that Sir Huntingdon and his wife were to have protection as they returned home.

After they left, His Highness turned once more to Brodie and me.

"I will send word to Lord Salisbery. For now, it is best that the other guests believe that it was an accident."

Brodie informed His Highness what we had learned so far, which was very little. However, two deaths in a matter of weeks? That first note and now another one?

Coincidence? Hardly, I thought. There could be no doubt that it was murder.

Obviously the two incidents were connected. But how? And what did it mean?

"It would seem, yer Highness, that young Salisbery's death was not due to robbery. Yet there is little to go on to find who is behind this." He picked up the note from the table.

And then there was one...

"Do ye know the meaning of it?"

"I have no idea..."

I caught the slight change in Brodie's manner. He didn't believe him. Neither did I.

"We canna help, sir, unless ye tell us everything ye may know of the matter. We would be wasting our time and yers. But I will tell ye this from experience, the person who wrote that note will not stop."

Strong words, perhaps stronger than most would dare use with His Highness.

"I will take the note and add it to wot we already know, but we should meet again tomorrow," Brodie continued.

The Prince of Wales nodded, his face heavily lined with exhaustion and the horror of the evening's events.

"You are right of course, Mr. Brodie. It should be in private, if possible, to avoid the newspapers learning of it. I will have Sir Knollys send round a message."

Aunt Antonia's driver, Mr. Hastings had taken her home earlier. He had returned and waited with the coach and four in the courtyard, along with her second driver.

He stepped down from atop the coach and waited until we had all stepped inside, then latched the door and climbed atop once more with instructions to take Brodie and me to the townhouse in Mayfair and then return to Sussex Square with Lily and Munro.

The coach lurched away from the entrance, then across the courtyard, and onto the roadway at the edge of St. James's Park.

"It was no accident." Lily repeated what she had told me earlier. "I know what I saw. That man pushed that young man over the railing."

"I believe ye, lass," Brodie replied through the shadows inside the coach. "It would seem there is more His Highness hasn't told us."

We rose early the next morning and immediately went to the office on The Strand.

Lily and Munro had returned to Sussex Square after leaving Mayfair the night before. Brodie had asked her to join us at the office this morning to share anything else she might remember from the events of the previous evening.

We had learned before parting that Munro had seen the shadowy figure of a man hurrying toward the queue of coaches but thought it one of the guests leaving the festivities, as several others had already.

He discovered that it was not one of the guests when he encountered Lily. He did seem a bit put off by that as he explained it.

Suddenly overcome with laughter, I had smothered it back in light of the evening's dreadful turn until my eyes watered at the image of Munro overcome by Lily who weighed no more than seven stone.

"I dropped ye on yer arse, when ye came from behind me," she clarified so there was no misunderstanding. "Ye're lucky I didn't use the knife on ye," she added.

"A cake knife?" he replied, indignant, and made one of those typical Scottish sounds, not exactly a word, however the meaning quite clear.

"Perhaps ye remember something about the man that could be useful," Brodie suggested as Lily now sat across from me at my desk. My notebook was opened before me.

"Was he tall?" Brodie inquired. She shook her head.

"Not as tall as yerself or Mr. Munro." She was thoughtful. "Shorter than ye." She told me.

"Do ye remember the color of his hair or eyes?"

"His hair was brown, overlong at his collar and curled up. His eyes were grey."

"Are ye certain?"

She nodded. "I was as close as I am to Mikaela. He turned, surprised that I was there. There was an odd look in his eyes."

She thought about that. "Almost sad. But his expression was... Not angry, but something."

Sad. That seemed odd to me, as well.

"What else do ye remember?" Brodie asked.

"His face was square," she continued. "He had a high forehead and there was blood on his cheek as if that young man might have struck him."

"What sort of clothes was he wearing?" I asked.

"A plain coat and trousers, black, with a jumper under."

I looked over at Brodie with some surprise.

"What age do you think he might be?" I then asked.

This was always more difficult, depending on a person's circumstances.

"Perhaps forty years of age."

She was amazingly observant under very difficult circumstances. However, I shouldn't have been surprised. One of her tutors explained that she had memorized entire passages of text in her studies.

"Don't ye want to know about the man's limp?" Lily then asked.

A limp? I think we both must have stared at her in surprise.

"His left leg. When he ran, he sort of hopped across the green." She described the man, as best she could, considering it was dark and the green behind Marlborough House only lit by streetlights along the perimeter.

Afterward, we ate luncheon at the Public House to Miss Effie's delight. She had become quite fond of Lily. And we learned that she and Mr. Cavendish were planning a Christmas wedding at All Saint's Church.

"In the small chapel," she clarified, giddy as a schoolgirl. "And thanks to you for puttin' in a word for us with the vicar."

It was a reminder that I had promised that Brodie and I would stand up for them for the ceremony.

"I've been thinking," I told Brodie as we returned to the office after midday meal. "Linnie is quite good with charcoal and paper. She always sketches out her paintings before she begins a painting. She might be able to create a drawing of the man from Lily's description."

"It could be useful," he agreed.

My sister had moved from the house at St. James's after her divorce, a sad affair, and I had been concerned she might simply retreat into her paintings and not wed again.

I had introduced her to my publisher, James Warren, after the release of one of my "Emma books." Then, while off on a recent case with Brodie, my great aunt informed me that there was "something going on there" between them.

"Thick as thieves," she'd explained. "Whenever I call to invite her to Sussex Square, she is not available. And then one of her servants mentioned Mr. Warren's name. Scandalous so soon after her divorce," Aunt Antonia declared with a wicked gleam in her eyes.

They were wed shortly thereafter, and my niece, Catherine, with all that red hair, was born a scant eight months later.

Scandal, scandal!

As if that was the first time something like that had ever happened among the ton of London society.

I was thrilled for my sister. Not only was she in love and now had a family of her own, but James had encouraged her to return to her painting, which she had previously been forced to give up.

We had traveled together for her Paris exhibit shortly before Catherine was born. I emphasize the word "shortly," as she gave birth to her less than a day after our return to London.

Catherine was now babbling in her own language, crawling all over the place, and asserting that bold, independent red-headed spirit to the point that Linnie had declared that she might be an only child. For his part, my brother-in-law James had announced that he would like a half dozen.

"Of course. I would be happy to assist," Linnie replied now over the telephone when I put through a call to her.

"And Lily? Marvelous!"

I thought I heard the distinctive sound of something crashing to the floor in the background.

"Oh dear, Cappy..." her father's nickname for young Catherine.

It seemed that she had just dragged down a vase of flowers and was squealing with delight among the ruins of vase and scattered blossoms.

"I will be expecting you," Linnie said in a rush and the conversation abruptly ended as she was then off to chase down her daughter.

As Lily and I prepared to set off for Kensington Place, where Linnie and James lived, Brodie penned a message to be delivered to HRH at Marlborough House. He was then hoping to meet with Mr. Dooley regarding the events of the previous evening.

"I will see ye after," he said in parting. "It will be interesting to see what yer sister is able to come up with from Lily's description."

Kensington Place, where my sister lived with her husband and daughter, was not the ostentatious manor where she had once lived as Lady Litton, during her first marriage that had ended so badly.

She refused to live in it after her divorce, with unpleasant memories, and had returned to Sussex Square to live with our great aunt for a time after that horrible experience.

The house at Kensington Place became available through a connection of our great aunt's and Linnie had purchased it.

It was quaint by comparison to her first residence, merely a half dozen private bedrooms, more than enough for six children. It included a library, garden room, parlor, and servants' quarters for her housekeeper and the nanny, in a red-brick blend of Georgian and Edwardian designs.

It was surrounded by trees with a garden behind a wrought iron fence. In summer, was filled with hydrangea blossoms. There was a pony shed at the back of the property that I suspected had more to do with her decision to purchase the house, as we once had ponies as children.

James had moved from his townhouse after they married and they had spent the following months settling into their new home and preparing for Catherine's arrival. She had furnished the nursery and had carpet installed over the planked wood floors, in case Catherine fell, along with several pieces of furniture and the installation of electric lighting.

She had converted the garden room into her artist's gallery where she had set up an easel with her current work in progress. A cabinet filled one entire wall that contained her art supplies, including canvas already stretched over wood frames for additional projects.

Her housekeeper, Mrs. Finch, met us at the door.

"Lady Lenore has just put Miss Catherine down for her afternoon nap," she greeted us. "She will meet you in the garden room."

The change in my sister, since her marriage and now motherhood, was remarkable. She arrived dressed in a morning gown with a full apron over, wisps of her blonde hair that favored our mother in disarray, her cheeks flushed, and announced that Catherine now had two more teeth.

"She is growing so fast...I finally persuaded her that she should take nap. Of course, it didn't hurt that she has a new favorite stuffed toy that James bought for her.

"Now you must tell me what this visit is about," she continued.

I had explained earlier that it was regarding an inquiry case and that Lily had seen someone who might be important to the case. I left out a few other details, such as the reason Brodie and I were there after first meeting with the Prince of Wales regarding that incident outside the gentlemen's club.

Linnie proceeded to take a large tablet of drawing paper from a drawer in the cabinet, along with charcoal pencils that I had seen her use before when sketching out ideas for a portrait or landscape.

She sat in the chair she usually occupied when painting, that sheet of paper clipped to the easel as Lily stood just behind her, and they began.

Lily repeated what she had told Brodie and me about the man she saw, with Linnie making sketches, then changes as Lily decided that something was not quite right. My sister was patient, working with the changes, until Lily nodded with approval.

"That's the man I saw," she announced.

Catherine had wakened some time earlier, and I had taken over nanny duties at the risk of being anointed with drool or some other substance that came with infants.

I had made a game of rolling a ball across the nursery floor for her. She'd crawled after, chattering away, telling me all about it, I was certain. She then grinned when she captured the ball and provided a full view of her new teeth.

Now, I juggled her on my hip as Linnie turned the drawing for me to see. It was amazingly life-like, complete with a mark on his cheek where Lily mentioned the man might have been struck by young Mr. Huntingdon.

"You're certain?" I asked Lily as I handed a squirming Catherine back to my sister.

She nodded. "That is the man I saw."

Seven

"MR. BRODIE RECEIVED a note a short while ago," Mr. Cavendish informed me as our coach arrived back at the office on The Strand after our visit with my sister.

"It looked official, hand-carried by a gentleman's man. Inspector Dooley came round earlier, and Mr. Munro is up at the office as well," he added.

I tucked the artist's tube with that charcoal drawing under my arm, and Lily and I headed for the lift.

Brodie looked up as we entered the office. Munro stood beside the cast iron stove where a fire glowed warmly. I did notice the frown on Munro's face as he acknowledged both of us.

"Good that ye're here," Brodie greeted us. "Ye will want to read this."

He handed me the note he had received with a royal crest on the accompanying envelope as I laid the tube with that drawing on his desk.

We were to meet with the Prince of Wales this very same evening at Marlborough House.

"Mr. Cavendish said that Mr. Dooley was here earlier?"

He nodded. "I tried to arrange for us to inspect the body of the young man. But it seems that the family has already claimed the body and made the necessary arrangements for burial."

That seemed rather sudden. There was usually a lying-in period at the family residence that often went on for some time. Aunt Antonia had mentioned one of her peers being "presented" as she called it in the family residence for thirty days. I had always considered that to be excessive.

"Even with the poor thing full of embalming fluids, she swelled up like a bloated fish and smelled like one as well. Yet, I will admit that I had noticed that about her when she was still alive," my great aunt had exclaimed at the time. "I say, put the poor thing in the ground and be done with it!"

I was inclined to agree and believe that had influenced her decision to go out in a Viking longboat set afire. A blaze of glory, as it were.

"Far more efficient," she had declared at the time. "And quite exciting, don't you think?"

My sister was not at all surprised when she heard of it afterward.

"Of course," she had remarked. "I would expect no less. She has been quite unconventional all of her life. Perhaps she should put in an order for two, you are quite like her, you know."

Yes, well...

"And we're to meet at Marlborough House?" I asked, returning to the subject at hand, namely that note.

"It seems that after the incident last night with the police called out by one of the staff, all information is now to be directed to Sir Avery at the Agency."

Of course, I thought. The Queen's man was now to take the case.

"Yet His Highness still wants to meet with us?"

"I suppose that it would be to discuss any other information we've been able to learn." He glanced down at the artist's tube at his desk.

"And this?" he inquired.

"It's the sketch Lady Lenore made from my description of the man I saw last night," Lily explained.

"A sketch?" Munro commented. "And ye saw the man?"

"It was very brief," Lily explained. "And then he was gone, but it could be helpful."

Brodie opened the tube, pulled out the charcoal drawing, then unrolled the sketch and spread it across the desk. He looked up at Lily.

"This is the man ye saw?"

She nodded. "Miss Lenore had a go at it several times, but that is verra near wot he looks like."

Brodie studied the sketch, then looked over at me. "Do ye recognize the man?"

I did not. Whoever he was, he was not among those I had seen that night; however with the number of people there, it was not surprising.

He nodded. "This could be useful. At least we know what the blighter looks like and with yer other details about him," he looked over at Lily, "the authorities and Sir Avery's people will know what to look for. Ye've done well," he told her.

With that, we prepared to leave for that meeting the Prince of Wales.

"Ye'll see the lass back to Sussex Square?" Brodie inquired of Munro.

He nodded. "Unless she has a notion to stop in the East End and take up the search for the man there?" he replied.

I exchanged a look with Brodie. That did seem a bit sharp.

"If ye dinna mind, Mr. Brodie, I would like to attend the meeting with ye. His Highness may have questions about the drawing," Lily pointed out.

She had a very valid point, in spite of Munro's comment. None of us had seen the man, and there might very well be questions about the drawing that we would not be able to answer.

I looked over at her. So many changes since she'd arrived from Edinburgh, along with that reminder from Brodie that she had matured a great deal since then. She was extremely intelligent, self-confident, and was quite determined to have her own way in things. The word there was stubborn. Not that I hadn't heard that before about myself.

"Ye canna change her," Brodie told me at the time. "Ye should well know that."

He was right, of course, and I had become very aware in the past year that she was determined to make her own way, no matter what I or anyone thought or said. That shoe was now on the other foot, as the saying went...

"Of course you should accompany us," I replied, much to Munro's obvious disapproval, though he did not say it. However, a Scottish sound was worth a hundred words.

"I'll go with ye as well," he announced. "Then I can escort the chit back to Sussex Square."

I caught Lily's reaction at being thought of as no more than a wayward child— that sudden lift of a dark brow, and the set of her chin. There was most definitely trouble there between the two.

.   .   .

Much like that previous evening at Marlborough House, the grounds and the mansion itself were well lit.

There were now substantially more guards at the entrance to the park surrounding the formal residence that also served as the formal office of the Prince of Wales.

Another set of guards waited at the entrance to the court-yard, with still more royal guards at the main entrance. I was not the only one to notice the increased presence.

"I've never seen so many," Lily commented.

Brodie had brought the sketch my sister made from Lily's description of the man she saw and chased that previous evening. And I had brought my notebook along with that note that was found on the young man's body, along with the first note that was found on the body of the son of Lord Salisbery.

We had discussed what we knew before leaving the office, along with several aspects that we could only speculate on.

There were now two deaths of sons of prominent members of the peerage, and three notes, one left on each of the bodies, and the last one with that cryptic message.

"And then there were two..."

We were met by Sir Knollys, the Prince of Wales personal secretary, at the main entrance to Marlborough House.

"Am I supposed to bow or curtsy?" Lily whispered as we followed him to the library that also served as the office for His Highness, where he conducted official business of the Crown, and on behalf of the Queen.

The walls were covered with portraits, including one of Prince Albert, his father, and another of the Queen hanging on the wall between those two arches. His desk was enormous, although it was difficult to see much detail because of the mountain of papers that covered it.

Over the hearth was a portrait of His Highness in a naval

uniform from his earlier years with the Royal Navy, while about the room, on a side table below a set of windows and at shelves that lined the other walls, was a collection of artifacts from places he had traveled.

We were greeted first by a scruffy terrier that leaped up and charged over to greet us as we entered the library.

"There now, Ulysses," His Highness called out.

The name did seem a bit misplaced for one so small.

The dog was far more obedient than Rupert, the hound who occupied the alcove below our office. It was obvious that Ulysses was immediately taken with Lily.

She reached down and scratched the dog's ears and told him what a good boy he was. When he'd received the attention he was after, Ulysses returned to sit by the desk of the Prince of Wales who stood as we arrived.

"Lady Forsythe and Mr. Brodie, I do appreciate you meeting with me this time in the evening."

Brodie nodded. "Aye, yer note explained the circumstance, sir."

"Please, be seated," His Highness said then. "We are past any formalities in this matter."

We sat before the hearth, Lily as well, although Munro chose to remain just outside the study.

Sir Knollys had one of the servants provide coffee, then left at a nod from His Highness.

"The past twenty-four hours have been...exceedingly difficult, as you may imagine," Prince Edward said as he set his cup aside.

"It has been most upsetting for my family and that of Sir Huntingdon. There are many questions, and I have requested this meeting due to a recent development that I had hoped to avoid.

"However, it seems that is not to be…particularly now with the Agency asked to make inquiries on behalf of the Queen. You should know that it was not of my choosing, as you have provided most excellent results in past matters."

"Sir," Brodie politely interrupted. "There are things we have been able to learn and would make that information available to Sir Avery."

"You perhaps misunderstand my intentions, Mr. Brodie," the Prince of Wales interjected.

"In spite of this 'development'," he added with no effort to disguise his displeasure, "I am not ending our arrangement."

I was surprised at his announcement as was Brodie.

It was no secret that there was a certain "estrangement" between the Queen and the Prince of Wales. It was rumored they rarely spoke.

According to my great aunt, he had been quite rebellious in his youth, something I understood well.

"Quite the contrary," he continued now. "I want you to continue. There will be the usual sensationalized publicity. There is no preventing that now. I am requesting that you both continue."

"Is Sir Avery aware of the notes that were received?" Brodie inquired.

I caught the hesitation on the part of His Highness.

"He is not. However, that will undoubtedly change very shortly."

Brodie was thoughtful.

"If we are to continue, sir, with what we've learned, we must have full control over our inquiries…with no interference. Guaranteed by Yer Highness."

It was a bold request that had the potential to put us in direct conflict with Sir Avery. However, His Highness nodded.

"Agreed."

"Any information that we uncover is to be seen only by yerself until the matter is resolved," Brodie insisted.

Once more, the Prince of Wales agreed to his request.

"And ye are to provide information regarding any clues that we find."

"Agreed, as well."

"We do not work for Sir Avery," Brodie insisted. "That must be made clear, nor will we report to him. I will not have him standin' over us or expectin' reports or updates."

"You know the man well," His Highness commented.

"Yer word on it, sir," Brodie insisted.

"You have it. You will answer only to me."

Brodie seemed satisfied with that.

"Ye may tell Sir Avery whatever ye wish of the arrangement, or not," Brodie said then. "But I will not be stepping over the man every minute. If it comes to that, then we will provide whatever information we have in the matter to ye and be done with it."

"Understood," Prince Edward replied with a faint smile. "Would you care for me to put that in writing, Mr. Brodie?"

I could tell that Brodie wasn't prepared for that, just as His Highness undoubtedly was not prepared to be lectured regarding the terms of our service. I also sensed from his expression that Brodie had apparently hoped that this would be the end of our involvement with the investigation and we would be on our way.

"What of the sketch?" Lily whispered.

"There is a matter that needs your attention," I entered the conversation since it seemed that, at least for the present, the two had reached an agreement. Even though I agreed with Brodie regarding Sir Avery.

I had no fondness for the man after previous circumstances, even if he was the Queen's preferred agent in the matter. He was too willing to sacrifice a person in the interest of solving a crime, and at one time that person was the man I was now married to.

"We had a sketch made from Lily's observations of the man she encountered last evening," I explained. "And with your permission...?"

"Of course, Lady Forsythe, please continue," His Highness replied.

I removed the sketch from the tube, laid it on a side table to prevent it being lost among the sea of paperwork as his desk, then nodded for Lily to explain the drawing.

She unrolled the sketch and blocked the four corners with objects she found there, with one corner remaining.

Prince Edward handed an ashtray to her. "Will this do, miss?" he inquired.

She set it onto the fourth corner of the drawing.

"This is the man you thought that you saw last night?" he inquired as he rounded the table to look more closely at the sketch. "In a matter of a few seconds after he sent that young man over the railing? A most difficult situation. And you then went after him across the green with only the light of gas lamps around the park?" he commented.

Anyone else might have been intimidated. As I say, anyone else...

"He looked at me from only a foot away," Lily replied, matter of fact. "That is the man I saw." She could be quite direct.

That took His Highness back a bit. When I would have said something in support of her, Brodie shook his head.

"I know wot I saw...sir," she added. "I see no reason to

bandy about something, particularly something as dreadful as wot happened to that poor young man."

"Indeed," he replied. "You have a point Miss…?"

"Lily Montgomery, sir," she replied.

"Montgomery. Of course," he acknowledged. "And an eye for detail so it seems."

"Do ye perhaps recognize the person in the sketch?" Brodie asked. "He was able to easily access Marlborough House that night. Might it be someone of yer acquaintance?"

Prince Edward studied the drawing.

I thought I saw something in his expression, not recognition but a thought that was there, then gone.

"No, I do recognize the man."

"I would like permission to show the drawing to Sir Knollys and other staff," Brodie then informed him.

"Of course. I will send for him and have him arrange for you to meet with whomever you wish."

"That does raise the point of Sir Avery's involvement now."

"Yes?" Prince Edward replied, then looked across the table to both Brodie and me. "I'm aware that you have worked with the man in the past."

I looked over at Brodie. I did wonder how he would choose to respond.

"Aye, in another matter. However, we have chosen to conduct inquiries on behalf of our own clients."

Prince Edward was thoughtful.

"Continue."

"I would have yer written authorization to make our inquiries, so that there is no confusion," he explained.

"You shall have it, in writing. I will direct Sir Knollys to draft it before you depart."

Brodie nodded and thanked him.

"There is the matter of the note that was found last night."

I retrieved the note and handed it to him.

"*And then there were two.* It would seem to have a specific meaning, now with the deaths of the two young men and the murderer's reference to them."

What did I see now in His Royal Highness's expression?

"And the first note?" I inquired. "*The sins of the father will be visited upon the children?*"

"I have no way of knowing," he replied somewhat dismissive, I thought.

"Obviously some cruel joke and all the more reason you must continue and find the person who is responsible."

Eight

BRODIE RETURNED to Marlborough House the next morning with the drawing my sister had made of the man Lily saw the night the son of Sir Huntingdon was attacked. Lily had spent the previous night at the townhouse in Mayfair and we prepared to leave for Sussex Square.

I wanted to learn more about something Aunt Antonia had mentioned about the Prince of Wales's reputation as a younger man and that somewhat unusual title that he and his university friends had been given.

It was a windy, wet morning, with clouds heavy with rain overhead. The rain grew heavier as Lily and I departed the townhouse.

I was not at all pleased about the outcome of our conversation with His Royal Highness the previous evening, informing us that Sir Avery Stanton was now making inquiries at the request of the Queen.

Even with HRH's assurances that he would intervene in the matter, I was not convinced that we should continue. Still, I had deferred to Brodie. It was, after all, his past experience with the Agency that had caused his refusal to work with them further at this time.

"Ye're not pleased about His Highness's request to continue with your inquiries," Lily astutely observed, no doubt due to the less-than-subtle conversation between Brodie and myself the previous evening upon returning to the townhouse.

"There was a difficult situation previously…" I chose not to get into details at the time.

"Ye do not trust Sir Avery," she concluded, quite perceptive.

"People often have other motives," I replied.

"And they can be dangerous?"

As I said, most perceptive.

It had been a situation where I deferred to Brodie's judgment in the matter even though I strongly disagreed. And it could have ended very badly for him after interference from Sir Avery.

Now, here we were again, pulled into a situation where we might once again find ourselves at cross-purposes with the man that might well cause extreme difficulty between His Highness and the Queen, when it was the murder of two young men that was most important.

Brodie knew my misgivings, not unlike his own. We had finished our somewhat heated discussion the previous evening, with his comment, "I know yer feelin's in the matter, but I've given my word to His Highness, and we have his written authorization to continue. If there is a conflict, we will end our part in it. If ye've a mind to refuse to participate, I understand."

He knew very well that I would not refuse.

Bloody, stubborn Scot.

. . .

Mr. Symons, my great aunt's head butler, greeted Lily and I as we arrived at Sussex Square.

"Her ladyship is in the solar this morning, Miss Mikaela. With Mr. Arneson, this morning."

"The ship builder!" Lily exclaimed with some excitement as we reached the solar and were greeted by my great aunt.

"Here you are!" she exclaimed. "What do you think of this design?"

The "design" was a drawing of a Viking longboat, made of wood, long—of course, with an enormous dragon's head at the helm, arched tail at the rear, a mast with a sail, and oars. The dimensions were written just below the drawing. It was to be over thirty feet long.

It was quite impressive.

"Going somewhere, are we?" I commented.

"I do believe one must be prepared," she replied. "Now, I need to decide where I will have it launched when the time comes, and the sail must have the design of my ancestor's banner," she added.

That, of course, was William of Normandy, William the Conqueror, the first king of England and a direct ancestor.

Our family had been in England for several generations, yet at the time I learned of it I admittedly thought her stories about that particular ancestor were an exaggeration.

That is, until I was older and discovered the "family" archive in the library which clearly proved that she was in fact a descendant of that somewhat notorious king who had arrived from France in 1066 to pillage the island.

"I do believe that we have a banner around here some-where," she explained to the boatwright, who managed to maintain a serious demeanor as I was certain he didn't usually receive a commission for a Viking longboat.

"It may perhaps be in the old part of the house," she added. "I will see that you have it for the sailmaker."

"Of course, madame."

"One must always be prepared," she explained after he left. "Agnes Moorpark dropped dead without leaving any instructions, and her three sons squabbled for weeks.

"There she was, laid out in a casket after the usual mourning period, turning a definite shade of green, as they were not in agreement if she should be embalmed. It was very near another month before a decision was made, and there she was moldering in their front parlor. I will not be moldering in the front parlor," she added emphatically, then smiled.

"How are you this morning, dear?" She looked past both of us. "Brodie is not with you?"

"He's at Marlborough House to question the staff about that young man's murder," Lily shared.

"Such an unfortunate situation," Aunt Antonia commiserated. "I understand that the Queen is most upset over the matter and called in Sir Avery."

I was not surprised that my aunt already had the latest inside word regarding goings-on at Buckingham Palace. She did have her circle of friends from among several well-placed families, which also included one of the Queen's ladies-in-waiting.

"I am surprised that you did not accompany Brodie." She motioned for one of the servants who had brought a serving tray with coffee and scones to put the tray on the table near the hearth.

After the servant had departed, I reminded her that she had mentioned the Prince of Wales's earlier exploits with his circle of friends from their university days. She poured coffee.

"The gossip was most entertaining," she said as she sat and gathered her satin robe around her.

"There was the tale about the alligator one of the young men managed to bring to university. It was a small one, yet it apparently created quite a bit of excitement when it was discovered in the headmaster's office. It reminds me of your friend, Templeton, and her lizard."

Said lizard was in fact a four-foot-long iguana Templeton had named Ziggy, a gift from an admirer after one of her tours.

Ziggy now resided at the London Zoo after he was accused of absconding with the pet of an acquaintance, even though he had a preference for roses and other plants over small dogs.

"I suppose the gossip was more the usual sort of things young men do at university," she continued. "There was the usual episode of sneaking off into the city and indulging in gambling, women, and other escapades.

"Then there was the rumor of the young woman who was found in one of the young men's off-campus accommodations, a tavern that several had taken over in some celebration or other.

"As I remember it, one of the young men was very near turned out from the university over the incident. Come to think of it, that was very near same time that His Highness's father, Prince Albert, traveled there quite abruptly and his son departed shortly after for service with the military.

"After that particular episode I don't recall that the Four Horsemen were mentioned again."

Most interesting. And now over thirty years later, two young men who were sons of two members of that somewhat notorious "brotherhood," were dead.

"You will be continuing with this new inquiry?" Aunt Antonia added.

"His Highness has requested it," I replied.

"Do be careful, dear. You and Mr. Brodie, of course.

Pursuing something of this nature can reveal things that certain people might not want known."

I had thought of that as well.

Everyone had secrets. Things that might be dangerous if the truth was known. We had encountered that in past inquiry cases.

In speaking with her, I now knew somewhat more about the men who had once been known as the Four Horsemen. While I didn't know a great deal about their sons, that original note now seemed quite threatening—*Sins of the Fathers will be visited upon their sons...*

A threat? But from whom? Someone who merely sought attention or perhaps blackmail, as was frequently the case when it involved someone of position.

Yet, as far as we knew, there had been no demand for payment. Then, what could be the motive?

Perhaps Brodie would learn something from among the staff at Marlborough House. Something that someone saw that might be helpful.

And then there would be the need to speak with the young man's father. Not a pleasant prospect, yet necessary if anything was known by the family before that attack.

I kissed her on the cheek, then stood.

"You're leaving so soon?" Aunt Antonia remarked.

"I might be able to learn something from the archive at the dailies that could be useful."

I had used the newspaper archives for past inquiries. If the scandal sheets from 1861 had carried write-ups about the deeds of the four young men, there might be something useful there.

"I'll go with ye," Lily commented. "Two pairs of eyes will make it easier."

It did seem as if we had acquired a new partner for our inquiries...

~

BRODIE

His Highness's personal secretary, Sir Knollys, had provided a room adjacent to the library at Marlborough House for the purpose of his meeting with those who had been present the night of the murder.

"Will this suit your needs, Mr. Brodie?" he had asked with a hint of what might have been disapproval that Brodie had experienced in the past in other places. That spoke of the differences in their social classes. It was something else that was not there when Mikaela was present.

"Quite well, Sir Knollys," he assured him as he waited for the next person to arrive from a list that Mikaela had provided of those most likely to have been present the night of the murder.

It was possible that one of them might have seen something or had an exchange with the murderer, who appeared to have moved easily among the guests.

That was over two hours ago he noted by the pocket watch he now carried, a birthday gift from Mikaela, although he didn't know precisely when his birthday was.

His only memory of it was a small celebration with a piece of sponge cake with jam that his mother had given him along with an unexpected gift when he was young. She had taken the money used for coal in the flat where they lived to purchase a pair of pants and boots for him.

They were not new, of course, purchased from the second's

shop near where they lived. But they were new to him, and there had been sponge cake.

It was slightly stale, purchased from the bake shop at the end of day. He'd paid no mind to the staleness of it with the sweetness of the jam.

Now, he enjoyed fresh sponge cake baked by Mikaela's housekeeper Mrs. Ryan. With any left after saved for the hound. It was that sort of contrast that caught him unawares at times—how far he'd come. Yet, there were still moments when what and who he'd been were there.

It clawed its way back to the surface, reminding him that he was no better than any other man on the street, with his own secrets, pain from the past, and a darkness inside.

Then, Mikaela was there, filling up the empty places inside him, soothing the darkness with her intelligence, stubbornness and sass, and other things that came with just a look.

It was a reminder that, as much as they came from different places and different circumstances, she understood the dark places that were there inside him in a way no one else could.

He looked up from the table that had been provided and the notepad he always carried.

Aye, sass, he thought with a smile as he waited for the Lord Steward of Marlborough House, a man by the name of Burgess, who had been with the household of the Prince of Wales for several years.

He had been in charge of staff and servants the night of the birthday celebration and had been present throughout the day and evening should a member of the royal family have a need.

It was possible that he might have seen the man whose likeness Lady Lenore had sketched from Lily's description.

He stood beside the table where he'd placed the sketch so that the man would see it straight away. Much the same as he had when he was an inspector with the MET and placed a piece of evidence where it could be easily seen by those he questioned and perhaps bring a reaction.

It might help Mr. Burgess remember an encounter with the man that evening—that in itself might reveal something important.

He looked up then as the man arrived. He wore a formal suit of clothes: coat, white shirt with cravat and striped charcoal trousers. His face was devoid of expression.

"Good morning, sir," the man greeted him. "I am Mr. Burgess, Steward at Marlborough House. His Royal Highness has informed me that I am to provide all cooperation for your visit."

He caught Burgess's glance at the sketch, then the quick glance at him.

Most interesting, Brodie thought. Had the man recognized the person in the sketch? It perhaps meant nothing. Or something?

"I appreciate His Highness's assistance in the matter," he replied. "Shall we begin?"

Speaking with a good number of people was always a tedious, time-consuming task. However, Mr. Burgess was able to shorten the matter by providing a list of servants who were present among the guests on the main floor that night in the usual performance of their duties for such an event.

The hours passed as, one by one, those summoned appeared, studied the sketch and then answered his questions.

Did they recognize the man in the sketch? Do they remember seeing anyone that resembled him that night? Was there anything that night that seemed unusual among the guests? Perhaps someone seen some place where they shouldn't have been?

The answers were invariably the same. No one had seen anything unusual, although more than one mentioned that it might be impossible to see any particular person with so many guests about.

Yet, more than one mentioned the upset when the young man fell from the balustrade on the second floor.

"Did ye perhaps see anything unusual sometime other than the incident?" he repeatedly asked. It seemed that no one had seen anything other than the reaction among the guests.

He asked the last young man he questioned to inform Mr. Burgess that he wanted to inspect the place where the "accident." as it was called, had occurred.

He also wanted to speak with the head groomsman who was present the night of the attack on the young man. It was possible the servant might have seen something as the attacker fled the mansion with Lily in pursuit.

As Mr. Burgess was apparently delayed with some matter, Brodie left that small room beside the library. He tucked his notepad with those few notes that he'd made into his coat pocket, then made his way to the hall where the celebration had taken place.

There hadn't been an opportunity to inspect the location the evening of the incident.

The stairway and the landing were carpeted over marble, as was the hallway that led to other rooms where some guests had gathered that night. The balustrade where the young man had fallen looked down over the saloon below which had been filled with other guests that night.

The railing had held but had been loosened as the young man obviously struggled with his attacker, with several places where the wood post had splintered and threatened to give way.

The area had obviously been cleaned since that night, with traces of a carpet sweeper on the carpet that lined the hall, though repairs to the balustrade had obviously not been made yet.

He frowned at what appeared to be a stain on a decorative ironwork crossmember that connected an elaborate design to the wood.

He pulled his handkerchief from his pocket and wiped it across the ironwork. Although the stain had long since dried, it very much appeared to be blood.

"Do be careful sir."

An older man in that same uniform of royal staff cautioned.

"His Highness has ordered it repaired. The carpenter and his men were to see to it this morning, but they were needed elsewhere first. Repairs will be made today to prevent any further accidents."

An accident? An interesting choice of words. It did seem that, as far as the servants were concerned, that is what the situation was to be considered.

"Were ye here the evening of the accident?" Brodie inquired as he had not previously spoken with the man.

"I am steward of the second floor, sir. It is my responsibility to see that the servants complete their daily tasks at Marlborough House for His Highness and his family."

Brodie introduced himself and the reason he was there.

"Of course," the head steward replied. "We were informed that you would be arriving and making inquiries."

"When was this area last cleaned?"

"The morning after the celebration for His Highness's birthday, sir. Upon instructions by her Highness, the Princess of Wales."

Brodie nodded. That was not unexpected.

"Were ye present that evenin' when the accident occurred?"

"Only afterward, sir, when it became known what had happened, as there was quite an upset among the servants."

No help there if the man was telling the truth, which he had no reason to doubt.

"Did ye see anyone about who might not have seemed to be one of the guests and then fled after the accident?"

The man shook his head. "As I said, I was not present. It took me several moments to arrive after I heard sounds from the saloon below. A dreadful situation, if I may say, sir. Is there anything else?"

"That will be all. I thank ye for yer time."

Brodie slowly inspected the landing and the hallway at the balustrade where the "accident" had taken place.

The presence of dried blood would seem to be from that night. It was unfortunate, but not surprising, that nothing else was found that might tell him something since the area had already been cleaned.

He imagined what had taken place there, from the description Lily had provided—the startled guests as young Huntingdon had struggled with his attacker, the moment he had been overcome and had fallen, and the attacker had fled to the end of the hallway, then down the servants' stairs to the main floor.

Lily had gone after the man and followed him across the green to the stables and carriage park. Only one other person, a servant who served champagne to the guests, thought he might have seen the man in the sketch.

"It was just a glimpse and then he was gone."

A chance encounter that lasted only seconds, and then the man was gone.

What were young Huntingdon's thoughts as they struggled? Had he recognized his attacker. Was the other man injured in the confrontation?

Lily said that the killer seemed to favor his left leg. Or was it from a previous injury?

As Brodie knew from his own time on the streets, when it was over and he'd managed to send young Huntingdon over the balustrade to his death below, there would have been a moment, perhaps two, afterward when the attacker might have hesitated.

That was when Lily had come upon him.

Had he been afraid then that he might be caught? Or had there been no emotion at all, no remorse for the young man he'd just sent to his death?

There was one thing Brodie was certain of, the murder hadn't been random, for robbery or some other injustice. It had been deliberate. But for what reason? To send a message with that note? What did it mean?

There had been two deaths, apparently connected with those notes.

There was most definitely more to this than the Prince of Wales had shared with them.

He took a long look about for anything he might have missed, then returned downstairs to call on the head groom at the stables who might be able to tell him something about that night.

Nine

❧

THE STRAND

LILY AND I spent several hours at the Times newspaper archives. I was familiar with the archives from previous visits in other cases. Most past issues of the dailies had been archived on film with a cataloguing system by date and could be viewed on microfilm reading screens, much like a camera.

However, for far older issues, if they even still existed, it could be a long and tedious process with many dates no longer available due to loss or faded issues that were impossible to photograph.

Lily had accompanied me previously, yet that had been when she was somewhat younger, after first arriving in London, and had become easily bored with the search for information. This time was different.

She had a sharp mind, excellent memory and deductive quality, and certainly wasn't intimidated by some of the things she had encountered. No doubt owing to her somewhat precarious early years in an Edinburgh brothel.

Experience, as I knew only too well, was an excellent teacher and oftentimes a relentless task master.

I might have wished for her to be innocent of the things she had experienced. Yet, as my great aunt had once pointed out about myself after one of my adventuresome episodes, those experiences had made me who I was. I remembered what she said at the time of my adventure to a Greek Island, instead of a reprimand.

"I would not change a thing about you, dear girl, even if I could. You are intelligent. What you have experienced in the past has made you stronger because of it. I simply ask that after one of your adventures, you find your way back safely."

And I had, after several adventures, including the inquiry cases I now undertook with Brodie.

He accepted me as I was—strong-willed to be certain, somewhat rash at times, a troublesome baggage as he often called me. Yet he was someone who understood me as no one ever had. I could do no less for Lily.

I understood her, the quiet strength that hid a temper that could be quite intimidating, the wounds deep inside that we both carried for different reasons that were really not so very different. Along with a certain amount of stubbornness.

And so, we returned briefly to the office on The Strand and made the few notes we had discovered while I'd been at a reading machine while she retrieved the next roll of film only to determine that there was almost nothing to be learned.

"What does it mean?" she inquired as we arrived at the office. Then, as if to answer her own question, "There were other articles about members of the royal family, but all of it was about vacations at the Isle of Wight, train trips north to Scotland, someone who was decorated for something, but nothing written about any incidents while the Prince of Wales was at university."

We were able to find the film archive from the year 1861,

but there were several editions of the daily that were missing. Perhaps damaged editions that could not be salvaged. Or…

"Perhaps removed," I replied.

"Removed?"

"To prevent anyone reading it."

"For what reason?"

"Possibly to prevent scandal," I added, something I had been thinking on the way back to the office.

"Do ye believe the families of the young men might have had the articles removed?" Lily asked, that clever mind of hers working through the possibilities. "Perhaps the Queen?"

"I believe that certain people will go to great lengths to protect themselves or others."

Lily had gone to the chalkboard upon our return and made a brief note, *"missing information,"* along with a reference to the Prince of Wales's name.

"How will ye and Mr. Brodie learn if there is something connected to that missing information?"

I smiled to myself. She was already thinking about the next step.

"It may be necessary to meet with the Prince of Wales and ask the question."

After our adventure at the Times archive and our return to The Strand, I accompanied her back to Sussex Square.

"Ye will tell me what ye learn," she insisted as we parted in the foyer of the hall. "I want to help."

I had the distinct impression that if we didn't keep her informed, she might very well take herself off to make her own inquiries about the case.

"Of course, and if there is something you can assist with, I will let you know."

"Yer word on it?"

"Yes," I replied as I became aware that we were not alone in the foyer.

In that way that Munro came and went, often without a sound—no doubt from his days living on the streets with Brodie—he nodded a greeting, then informed Lily, "Her ladyship inquired if ye had returned."

I caught the brief change in her expression from our conversation to some other reaction at the reminder.

"Yes, of course, Mr. Munro," she replied somewhat frostily.

That was something different that I had noticed of late. They usually got along quite well. I did wonder if there had been a difficulty between them.

I caught the frown on Munro's face.

"Stubborn chit," he muttered after she left.

"Hmmm, yes," I commented. "However, she is hardly a child any longer."

That sharp blue gaze met mine. "Next, she'll be thinking of takin' herself off on some dangerous adventure."

There had obviously been some difficulty there.

"We cannot keep her here forever," I replied what Brodie had said to me. "And she does have that strong Scots temperament."

I could have sworn I heard a muttered curse as I departed.

Lights glowed along the streets as I returned to The Strand, and from the office windows on the second floor. With a single light that shone below the sign that had been recently added and announced, "Brodie and Forsythe Private Inquiries," even though it had met with some resistance.

"I dinna need a sign for people to know where we are. They find their way easily enough," Brodie had commented rather strongly when he first saw the signage, which was quite discreet without the usual garishness of some of the other signage along The Strand.

"It's not as if that fella over on Baker Street has a need to advertise his services."

It was a fact that most all of our inquiry cases came through people we knew or on the recommendation of others. Still, I thought it looked quite professional.

He did have a point. I would not be surprised to return to The Strand at some point and find the signage had been removed with the excuse that it was due to weather or the occasional sort who left somewhat colorful chalk messages on the sidewalks or on the front of buildings over some complaint.

"Mr. Brodie arrived a short while ago, and in somewhat of a temper," Mr. Cavendish informed me. "A warning, miss. It seems that he did not have an agreeable day."

Interesting.

"I was about to take meself over to the Public House for a bit of supper," Mr. Cavendish added as he guided the platform that he sat upon to the curb.

"I could bring a carton back," he suggested.

"No thank you." I replied. "We'll be along."

As I entered the office, I appreciated the warmth of the fire in the coal stove along with the bottle of Old Lodge whisky open on his desk, and the man who stood before the chalkboard where Lily had made our notes earlier.

So far it seemed safe enough, I thought as I smiled to myself and closed door behind me.

Then, without turning, without even the least acknowledgement, he gestured to the board.

"It seems that yer day might have been much the same as my own."

I approached where he stood before the board, took the glass from him and downed some of my great aunt's very fine whisky, from Old Lodge in the north of Scotland.

"And your inquiries at Marlborough House?" I inquired.

I went to the desk and refilled the glass, then handed it back to him.

"The Lord Steward arranged for me to speak with the people on the list ye gave me and several others. Only one man *thought* he recognized the man in the sketch, though he couldna be certain."

There was more.

"And His Highness's staff is to be commended. The landing where the man pitched young Huntingdon over the edge has been thoroughly cleaned of any unsightly matter."

"What of your conversation with the Master of the Stables? Did he see the man Lily went after?"

"It was dark, impossible to see anything more than the figure who ran past and then disappeared. And not a mention about a limp or difficulty as the man ran."

Once again, I was not surprised.

"Lily could have been mistaken."

He shook his head. "I trust Lily's word on it. But I did find something on the floor of the hall where the encounter took place."

He reached across the desk for the pipe that he smoked on occasion. He lit it, then sent a stream of fragrant smoke into the air towards the chalkboard.

"I found traces of blood on the balustrade. It seems that the young man might have been injured before he was sent over the rail."

I frowned. "There was no mention of a wound from His

Highness's physician who was there that night. It could have been from some previous situation."

"It did seem as if the fall itself was the cause of the young man's death."

"Aye."

"What are you thinking?"

"It could be important to see the young man's body. I made the request to His Highness's personal secretary. What of yer visit to the newspaper archives?"

I frowned. "There was no mention of the incident at Cambridge, nor that unusual title of the group of young men while students. There was a great deal of gossip about the fact that His Highness left the university just prior to Prince Albert's illness and death.

"One might almost think that any mention of incidents involving the group might have been removed from the copies filmed for the archive. And no original issues of the newspaper from those dates exists."

"Ye believe they may have been deliberately removed."

"It would not be the first time."

"And not mere gossip?" he added.

"I trust Aunt Antonia's memory of things. It can be almost frightening at times. Either that or she is clairvoyant." Which was a possibility.

I reminded him that his request to view young Huntingdon's body might very well be denied by the family or others.

"Her ladyship might have some influence in the matter," he pointed out.

I was not eager to involve my great aunt. It would only encourage her interest in our inquiry cases. Yet, he was right.

It was still early in the evening, and I placed a telephone call to Sussex Square.

"Of course, dear," Aunt Antonia replied when I explained the situation. "So unfortunate about the young man. Most certainly Sir Knollys can be somewhat difficult. He is the official gatekeeper for the Prince of Wales. I will speak with Sir Knollys over my concerns of rumors that are circulating about the situation, or something of that nature. I'll come up with something to move him along, as they say, with your request."

I did have the distinct impression as I ended the call that I might very well have opened Pandora's box in the matter.

Brodie had heard my part of the conversation. I caught a faint smile.

"We may very well regret it. You know how strong-minded she can be when she wants something."

"I've had some experience with that."

Ten

WE HAD STAYED over at the flat that adjoined the office for the night, after taking supper at the Public House across The Strand.

I had then spent the time after adding new questions to the blackboard.

It was late when Brodie had put more coal in the stove, and we had retired for the night.

Now, the telephone in the outer office woke us with that sharp jangling sound. Brodie cursed, then sprang from the bed, clad only in his underdrawers.

As I squinted through the light when he turned on the electric lamp, I was reminded that he was quite a stirring sight, most particularly in his underdrawers.

He cursed again, found his shirt, then quick-stepped bare-foot across the cold floor into the adjoining office as I buried my head into the warm covers.

I made out enough words to know that he was speaking with my great aunt.

It seems that she was out and about Sussex Square,

performing her morning routine of briskly walking about the gardens—part of her new routine to ward off the infirmities of old age and build her stamina. And before first light! It had to be against some law or rule.

She had spoken of a trip to Switzerland the coming year and was preparing to hike the Alps, something I hoped to persuade her against. All things considered I was not prepared to send her off in that longboat any time soon.

Brodie appeared at the doorway. "Her ladyship has some information."

Since I had only limited items of clothing at the flat, I wrapped the top blanket around myself and dragged it with me as I went to his desk.

"There you are, dear," Aunt Antonia greeted me. "Do forgive the early hour of the morning. I hope that I was not interrupting anything."

"Not at all," I assured her as Brodie returned and took the chair across. He now wore his trousers and an irresistible frown.

"I spoke with Edward last night, that is Sir Laughton," she began.

I knew Sir Laughton, her attorney, quite well. He had assisted Brodie and I in past matters. He had a thorough experience with the law and was held in high esteem by his peers, as well as my great aunt.

He had represented her in various legal matters including the appropriate documents for her to purchase the building on The Strand that she had then signed over to Brodie. She had declared, at the time, that she needed to do it before it slipped her mind or she took that final voyage in that Viking longboat.

However, it was the first time she referred to her attorney as *Edward*. It did seem as though there might be something there.

"I gave him the details of the situation," she continued. "He is quite well acquainted with Lord Salisbery and Sir Huntingdon and suggested that a formal note might be helpful. Especially regarding a legal aspect to do with obstructing an investigation or something like that, along with a directive that you are to be contacted immediately.

"Not to mention the gossip any reluctance on his part would cause. He thought that might take care of the matter and promised to dash off that formal request first thing this morning and have it delivered to you."

Her voice grew faint, and I thought we might have lost the connection amid much background noise.

"Lily has asked if she might join you when you make your observations of the body. Now, I must return to my hiking. Do say hello to Brodie."

And in keeping with her habit of simply leaving the call, I heard the clunk of the earpiece as she walked away.

"Mikaela?"

I recognized Lily's voice.

"I would like very much to join ye and Mr. Brodie when ye go to inspect the body." She waited expectantly before continuing.

"I have seen bodies before, and I'm no sissy pants to faint away at a little blood and a few bruises."

"I know you are not," I replied. "It's only that a mortuary is hardly the place for a young lady."

"Nor an older one?" she retorted.

I tried once more to dissuade her. "It can be quite gruesome."

"Loss of a limb? Worse? It's not as if I haven't seen that sort of thing before." She argued. "Ye see a lot of that on the streets,"

She had me there.

The call ended with Lily demanding a promise from me that we would let her accompany us to the mortuary where young Huntingdon's body had been taken.

"Congratulations, most commendable, Miss Forsythe," Brodie commented. "I expect to find her on our doorstep before mid-morning."

It was actually much closer to noon when Lily appeared on the landing to the office. She had dressed appropriately for the visit that had been arranged after Sir Laughton's note was sent to Sir Robert Huntingdon.

"You have today," the note we received said. "The lying-in period at the Huntingdon residence is to begin tomorrow," Sir Laughton had informed us less than an hour earlier.

I had immediately contacted Mr. Brimley, the chemist at the shop in the East End who had assisted us previously when it came to inspecting a body. He was to join us at the mortuary.

It was short notice to be certain. It had been two full days since young Huntingdon's death with his body to be sent to his parents' residence for the usual lying-in period.

I wasn't at all certain what Brodie hoped to find, but we were to meet Mr. Brimley at the mortuary St. James's at Westminster at one o'clock.

We arrived in good time and Mr. Brimley joined us shortly after. He had brought a leather carry bag that usually contained the instruments one might find in a physician's bag.

He had attended medical school in London. Instead of setting up a medical practice afterward, he chose to open his shop where he provided medicine and care for those in the East End who could not afford medical care.

He had taken care of more than one victim in the course of our inquiry cases, including myself.

He nodded good naturedly as if we were about to set off to market rather than enter a mortuary.

"Shall we get on with it, then?" Mr. Brimley inquired.

I supposed that all morgues were the same, very much like the one I had visited in a recent case in the East End. However, it was obvious that the "clientele" served here were of a far different class.

The entrance was much like a business office with fine furnishings, a carpet underfoot, and an attendant who greeted us in a very dignified tone.

"We were informed that you would be calling on us this afternoon," he acknowledged.

We were asked to wait while the attendant announced our arrival to a gentleman by the name of Hiram Bascomb, the mortician. It seemed that the private "grieving" salon was presently occupied.

"Is there a school for morticians?" Lily whispered. "Seems a strange profession."

I had to agree on that.

What would the course of study be? A course in body arrangement? Reattaching a stray body part on behalf of the bereaved? A hand or foot that had been severed? And then cosmetics applied that simply made the deceased appear barely recognizable.

Aunt Antonia had a far better solution to the whole thing with her Viking longboat.

The attendant promptly returned, and we followed a lady in a plain black gown who escorted us to the holding room.

In contrast to the outer office, waiting area, and the hallway that connected the two areas, the room where young Huntingdon had been taken was very much like the holding area for the Metropolitan Police that I had attended in the past.

It was immaculately clean with a half dozen compartments that lined the far wall, an examination table with a side table that contained the tools of the trade, as it were. Mr. Bascomb greeted us with somber propriety.

"I was informed of your request. Somewhat unusual I must say."

"We appreciate yer assistance on behalf of Sir Huntingdon and his family," Brodie replied.

"Of course," Mr. Bascomb replied with a faint smile that immediately disappeared as he turned and went to that far wall, opened one of the chambers, and then rolled out an examination table with young Huntingdon's body.

"A cold box?" Lily whispered. "Like Mrs. Ryan taking a partridge out for supper."

Yes, well, I couldn't fault her for that comparison.

"I was told to expect two of you," Mr. Bascomb sniffed with obvious disapproval.

"Mr. Brimley is an expert in such matters," Brodie explained. "The young lady is an associate of ours." Then added, "And thank ye for your assistance, sir."

When he had gone, Mr. Brimley set his bag on the steel cart nearby, then approached the examination table.

"Bruising about the neck," he began. "That would be consistent with the fall you described." He had donned rubber gloves, then continued, gently moving the head about.

"Neck broken in the fall as you can see by the odd angle." He then pulled back the sheet to the young man's waist and continued with his examination.

I glanced over at Lily. If she was shocked, I didn't see it.

Instead, she had taken a notepad from her carry bag along with a pen and was making notes of Mr. Brimley's observations the same as myself. If she was shocked or overwhelmed, I did not see it.

"There are other bruises and scrapes around the shoulders and arms that are to be expected as well from the fall you described," Mr. Brimley commented, then asked, "What else might you be looking for, Mr. Brodie?"

"Another wound perhaps."

Mr. Brimley rounded the table and then adjusted his glasses as he leaned in for a closer inspection.

"There is a mark here on the other shoulder and then lower across the *pectoralis major*." He looked up. "That would be the chest muscle, you see here," he pointed with a metal instrument that he'd taken from his bag.

"It's faint, but it's there, the skin has been broken as if the victim might have encountered something sharp. You did say there was a struggle."

He pointed to a mark on the shoulder that seemed to align perfectly with the mark on the young man's left chest muscle.

"It would seem that his attacker might have had a knife."

I had moved closer and added a diagram that I knew Brodie would want, illustrating the faint marks that did seem to faintly resemble a cross mark.

It was quite superficial and had not cut deeply. Yet, that might account for the blood Brodie had seen on the balustrade on the landing at Marlborough House.

Mr. Brimley continued his examination of the body for any other marks or wounds. It was no surprise that there were a good number of bruises.

"Blood will continue to make those marks under the skin for a short while even after death. That accounts for the bruising that you see," Mr. Brimley continued to explain.

"Unfortunate. So very young, just beginning his life."

"Is there anything else, you can tell us?" Brodie inquired.

"Everything I see is consistent with the fall you described."

"And the cut to the skin on the chest and shoulder?"

"Obviously a fresh mark, perhaps made if the young man fell against something in the course of the fall."

"Aye," Brodie replied with a thoughtful expression.

We had been there more than an hour by the clock at the wall and Mr. Bascomb had returned.

"Will that be all? May inform Sir Huntingdon that the matter is concluded?"

"Of course," Brodie replied, and thanked him.

"The poor man was so young," Lily commented after we found a driver and parted ways with Mr. Brimley. "Who would want to harm him?"

That was precisely what we needed to learn.

"What was meant by that note?" Lily then asked. "*'Now there are two?'* Two dead? Or that there will be two more murders?"

Eleven

CLEVER GIRL. I had thought the same about that note. It was a chilling prospect and made it all the more important that we find who was responsible.

But who? What was the motive?

I stood back from the chalkboard as I tried to make some sense of what we had learned.

We had returned to Mayfair the previous evening after our visit to the mortuary at St. James's. Lily had stayed over, and we had compared notes that we had each taken.

We had then taken supper, and she had retired for the evening, while Brodie and I discussed what we had learned that day.

We were still discussing it this morning at the office on The Strand after seeing Lily back to Sussex Square. She had handed me her notes before leaving.

"In case you missed anything Mr. Brimley found with his examination," she suggested.

Cheeky girl.

I hadn't missed anything when I compared our notes the

night before. But neither had Lily. She was very observant and quite thorough.

"Ye canna prevent her doing as she pleases," Brodie commented as we shared a second cup of coffee.

"It's only that I had hoped…"

His hand brushed mine. "That ye could protect her by providin' an education, and a fine place to live?"

It was that, but it was more.

"The options for young women are so antiquated and restrictive." I knew that as well as anyone. "They are expected to marry well, have several children, then quietly sit at home while their husbands are off carrying on with all sorts of ridiculous pursuits, or affairs."

"Yer sister seems to have married a good man," he pointed out.

"James Warren is an exception to be certain," I conceded. He was not titled but highly educated, hardworking, and not at all the sort to go off to his club, gambling away his home and family fortune, or causing scandals with his mistress.

I felt that dark gaze as he took another sip of coffee.

"And there is yerself," he commented. "When ye swore ye would never marry."

He knew the reasons. I had spoken of them. And here we were. A man from the streets with more honor than anyone I had ever known, someone I could trust.

"You were very highly recommended," I pointed out. I did have my great aunt to thank for that.

"I believe there was something about yer toes?" he replied.

I looked at him with some surprise. I had never spoken of that, something my great aunt had shared with me.

"Her ladyship might have mentioned it," he commented as he reached out and took my hand.

"And as for yourself, Mr. Brodie?"

He pulled me down onto his lap.

"It might have been yer red hair, natural the way it is, no chemicals or artificial color." He proceeded to pull the pins from it. "It might have been the way ye looked at me when ye were injured during that first inquiry, blood all over ye, and ye stood there like some avenging spirit. Or it could be the way ye refuse to give up on someone when it would be far easier to walk away."

"I believe you call it stubborn," I replied.

"Aye, there is that, and God knows ye have a wicked temper when ye get yer red up."

"Not the usual qualities one looks for in a wife," I admitted but refused to make any apologies.

His hand wrapped around mine.

"Or it could be that I wanted ye, more than I've ever wanted a thing in my life. In spite of that temper of yers and the habit ye have of getting yerself into things that ye shouldna that may be the death of me yet." He kissed my fingers.

"You seem to have survived quite well until now," I replied as I brushed my fingers across the beard on his cheek.

"Aye, until now," he replied with a that half smile that.

"What is to be done about Lily?" I asked. I did value his opinion on things, although we didn't always agree.

"It would seem that ye have two choices. Ye can ignore what is in front of yer eyes and attempt to keep her at Sussex Square with music lessons and whatever else it is that young ladies are taught. Knowin' full well that she will take herself off, possibly to some Greek Isle on an adventure."

That was not lost on me, as I had done that very thing, a few years older than Lily, but nevertheless...

"Or?" I inquired, most definitely uneasy about that possibility. Being a guardian most certainly had its drawbacks.

"Or," he continued, "ye might consider allowing her to pursue one of our cases. She does have a mind for details, good instincts from her own experiences, and spirit."

I knew that he was right. I could not simply leave Lily at Sussex Square where I knew she was safe and well-cared for, much like a favored pet. She most certainly had a mind of her own and would not hesitate to take herself off on some folly that could cause her harm.

"I will speak with her after our present inquiry, about perhaps assisting us from time to time on some of our simpler cases."

"She has already assisted us," he passed me, going to the wall beside the chalkboard where I had tacked up both our drawings of that mark on young Huntingdon's body.

"It couldna hurt to have her part of it now. If ye were to wait, she might decide to conduct her own investigation and get into some mischief."

The wisdom of the Inspector of Police that he had once been?

"You are right, of course," I replied with resignation.

The question was: what might that be.

I frowned. "I've been thinking that we do need to speak with the staff at the club where the son of Lord Salisbery was murdered. Someone there might have seen something as he was leaving."

"Go to White's? With Lily?"

"We would undoubtedly be refused entrance to the club, considering that it is for gentlemen 'only,'" I replied. "It could be an important lesson for her regarding some of the aspects of our cases."

I could see the objection in the way that dark gaze narrowed.

"A perfect suggestion for her to participate," I decided. "In the meantime, you can make inquiries with the Salisbery's personal physician who attended the young man before he was taken to the mortuary at St. James's." We had discussed that on our return from that place.

"There might be something the physician noticed about the body that could be helpful," I rose and went to the wall beside the chalkboard and studied the two drawings.

There was most definitely something peculiar about the marks. They were identical—Lily was the first to notice it. I couldn't help but think that I had seen something very similar.

We stayed the night at the flat next to the office. We rose early and I made a telephone call to Sussex Square to invite Lily to join me to call on White's private club. Even though I had little confidence that we would learn anything and might even be turned away. Such was the hallowed domain of gentlemen-only clubs around London.

She was to meet me at the townhouse, and we would continue from there.

Brodie had obtained the name of the physician who had attended to the son of Lord Salisbery when his body was discovered after the brutal murder that had occurred after he left White's.

Before I departed, Brodie handed me the note we had received from the Prince of Wales, requesting that we make inquiries into the matter with all due haste. It might assist in obtaining entrance into those hallowed walls.

We agreed to meet back at the office after our inquiries.

"Dinna let Lily go off by herself in the place," he cautioned. "Though I doubt there is anything she might see that would be surprisin', considerin' where she lived in Edinburgh. Still, with wot ye've taught her, along with her skill with a sword and other weapons, I wouldna want anyone to be run through for an inappropriate gesture."

Lily arrived promptly at the townhouse. I was somewhat surprised to see that she was accompanied by Munro. It appeared that she was not pleased.

"As if I am a child that needs an escort to make certain that I arrive safely," she had commented after being safely delivered. "I did not dare tell him where we were going. He would have accompanied us!" she added.

Instead, she "might have mentioned" that we were to go shopping at Harrod's and then have luncheon. He did look at me with some suspicion.

"He is verra much like an old woman." She shook her head after he left, that Scots accent from the streets of Edinburgh slipping through as it did when she was upset over something, or someone.

White's Club was at St. James's, on the near end of the street from where we were at the mortuary the day before.

It was imposing from the outside, set back from the street, five-stories of white cut stone with a slate roof, and occupied the double address of 37-38 St. James's Street.

It was an exclusive club for gentlemen of society and rumored to have several titled gentlemen, members of Parliament, and the Prince of Wales among its membership. However, that was not precisely known as that information was not for public knowledge.

I had previously been inside a men's club in another

inquiry case and knew what to expect as we stepped down from the coach and approached the main entrance.

Other than the street number 37-38, there was nothing to reveal that it was in fact a very exclusive club with rumors and gossip speculating over the activities that went on inside. Those included the usual card games, gambling, betting between members and guests, and of course, certain activities that went on discreetly in those rooms upstairs.

The fact that a woman might call on them could be for only one reason, and the doorman was quite surprised when I informed him that I wished to speak with the director of the club.

"Do you have an appointment?" he inquired after regaining his composure. "Miss...?" he added as an afterthought.

"Lady Forsythe, on behalf of our client."

There was the faint lift of the eyebrows, usually a result when I used my formal title.

"And your client would be?"

I presented him with one of our calling cards, tastefully printed with our names—Brodie and Forsythe—and the address of the office on The Strand, along with that note from His Highness. He stared at it.

"Are you going to leave us standing at the street?" I inquired in my best imitation of an affronted lady.

"No, it is only that...Brodie and Forsythe, Private Inquiries?" he read the card, then looked up at me. "That is unusual."

"I am certain Sir Barton-Fellowes would not care for this conversation to continue on the street," I added.

"Of course not, Lady Forsythe," he assured me more than a little surprised at the name I presented him as it was not well-known who the present chairman was at any given time. Another of those closely guarded secrets.

"Then, please let him know that we are here."

"Of course." He stood aside and we entered the foyer of White's.

"I will announce your arrival to the chairman."

I thanked him and he set off across what could have passed for an elegant front entrance of a palace.

"That is the first time I've heard you use your title," Lily whispered as we waited.

"Desperate moments require desperate measures," I replied.

Yet, it remained to be seen if my performance would achieve the meeting I hoped for.

"And you know the chairman's name?"

"There is usually more than one according to Aunt Antonia. She is somewhat an authority." I did not go into details.

"She is well acquainted with Sir Anthony, and I took a chance that he might be about." I did not go into details about her acquaintance with him either.

The attendant returned, somewhat contrite.

"Sir Barton-Fellowes will see you now. If you will follow me."

I caught the look Lily gave me and smiled.

"I must say, Lady Forsythe, this is somewhat of a surprise." Sir Barton-Fellowes rounded his desk in greeting and took my hand. "We don't normally have lady visitors."

I thanked him for meeting with us.

"And this young lady would be?" he inquired.

"Miss Lily Montgomery," I made the formal introduction.

"A very old and distinguished family," he replied with a curious look at Lily. She nodded with a polite smile.

"Please, do be seated." He indicated the chairs before the desk. He then returned to his desk. "Tell me what has brought you to White's."

"I do realize this is most unusual," I began, then explained the reason we were there.

"This is most unusual," the chairman commented. "You must understand, Lady Forsythe, that we are in no position to make any comment regarding a member of White's. Privacy is to be maintained at all times. I would think that any inquiries into the matter would be made directly to the family."

"Of course, and in due time," I replied. "However, I would like very much to speak with the footman who was here that night and would have summoned the coach for the young man."

He sat back at his chair. "That would be highly irregular."

"I understand, however anything he might remember from that night could be most helpful in bringing this matter to a close. I'm certain you understand the importance of that for Lord Salisbery and his family."

I then asked, "Is the footman who was here that night available?"

"That would be Mr. Masterson, a long-time employee of White's."

I caught the hesitation and sensed the refusal that would come next. I reached across the desk and laid the note from the Prince of Wales on the desktop in front of him.

"The Prince of Wales?" he exclaimed.

"He has asked us to make every effort in the matter to resolve this dreadful situation," I informed him.

Even though he was a gentleman for whom discretion and composure were paramount, I caught his reaction in the sudden tightening of his jaw as he read the note that Brodie had been given.

"I understand," he replied. "I will summon Mr. Masterson. You may meet with him here in my office. If you will wait, please." He then offered to have tea or coffee brought in while we waited.

"That will not be necessary," I politely replied. "We have an appointment afterward. I am certain you understand the urgency and that a particular person should not be kept waiting." I then pointedly retrieved the note and tucked it into my notebook.

Let him think what he would about whom that appointment was with.

"What appointment?" Lily whispered after he left the office. "With the Prince of Wales?"

I wouldn't have called it a lie, more of a hint that I had put out there so that we might be able to speak with the man.

"Ye let him believe that we would be meeting with the Prince of Wales," she continued to whisper with a look that could only be described as amazement. Then she smiled. "Quite clever."

The chairman returned expeditiously with an older gentleman whom he introduced as Mr. Masterson.

"Well done," Lily whispered.

BRODIE

The physician's office was on Harley Street, in a row of discreet red brick offices near the private hospital in Marylebone. This was information Mr. Dooley had provided from the official police investigation into the death of young Charles Holt-Densmore, the son of Lord Salisbery.

He was told Robert Chapman, physician, should be returning any time from an early morning visit to the hospital. The woman who appeared in the outer office, Mrs. Chapman, was polite and informed him that if it was a medical issue, he could find the doctor at the hospital

"Not at all," he thanked her. "It is a private matter."

And he waited and made a handful of observations about the good doctor from the certificates and commendations framed on the wall behind a desk.

Chapman had graduated from King's College according to a framed certificate, as well as a surgeon with honors from the University of Edinburgh Medical School. There were several other framed certificates, as well as one that noted his military service.

He was obviously well connected as there was also a photograph that included two other men, one notably Lord Salisbery, obviously at the hunt with a stag at their feet as they posed with rifles in hand.

Well educated, a man who had served with the military, obviously highly thought of, and the person Lord Salisbery had contacted when his son was brutally murdered. Would the man be willing to discuss the situation with him?

The answer to that came as the door opened. He turned and met the steady gaze of the man in that photograph.

Mrs. Chapman appeared and informed the doctor that he had been waiting to meet with him.

Brodie immediately caught the speculation in the man's expression as they had not previously met.

He provided his name and one of the calling cards he now carried.

"Professional Inquiry Service?" Dr. Chapman read the information on the card.

"In a private matter, sir," Brodie replied. "If ye please."

Dr. Chapman removed his great coat and neck scarf and indicated for him to take a chair across the desk. With a curious glance, his wife reminded him of a consultation he was to attend, then departed.

"In what way may I be of service, Mr. Brodie?"

"In the matter of the death of the son of Lord Salisbery."

He caught the guarded look that immediately appeared.

"A most tragic situation," Chapman replied. "You are here on behalf of the family?"

"On behalf of His Royal Highness," Brodie replied.

He would have preferred not to bring the Prince of Wales's name into it. Yet, he knew well enough that he might not have learned anything otherwise.

"He has asked us to make certain inquiries into the matter."

Dr. Chapman took a deep breath, his expression thoughtful with fingers steepled before him.

"You obviously would not make such a claim if it were not so, and risk arrest by the police," he commented.

"I was previously an inspector with the Metropolitan, sir. As I stated, I am making inquiries at his request, and ye are correct that I would not risk being arrested."

The man was careful, obviously protective of his patients, yet despite the fact that it might complicate this inquiry, Brodie liked the man. He was straightforward in his manner, and hopefully Brodie would be able to learn something in the matter of young Lord Salisbery's murder.

He felt that scrutiny, then the way the doctor's expression eased.

"How may I help you, Mr. Brodie?"

He spoke of the information in the police report and from the coachman that night, then asked his questions about the physician's part in the examination of the body afterward.

"Horrible situation," he described what he observed after he was called to the hospital by Lord Salisbery.

"There was extensive damage to the upper body, including internal organs." Dr. Chapman shook his head. "And the loss of a great deal of blood.

"So tragic," he added. "I knew the young man through my acquaintance with Lord Salisbery. I only wish that I could have helped him. And now I have heard of the death of a second young man?"

He was obviously well informed in spite of efforts to keep the murders out of the dailies.

"I learned of the death at Marlborough House." He was thoughtful. "You mentioned that you were previously with the MET. Has there been any development in the search for the those responsible for these dreadful situations?"

"That is the purpose of my visit, sir. With the hope that ye might be able to provide assistance."

"Of course, if there is any way that I can."

"Were there any unusual marks on the young man's body other than the wounds you have described?"

"Marks?" Dr. Chapman remarked. "There were several as I have already said. Any one of them might have caused death. The other wounds unnecessary, almost as if..."

"As if wot?" Brodie inquired.

"As a surgeon and in my time with the Queen's service, I have seen many wounds, but none made with such viciousness, with something very near fury, almost as if the attack was personal." He looked across his desk at Brodie.

"You must understand that is merely an impression."

Most interesting. Brodie nodded. "Please continue."

He took the sketch Mikaela had made at the mortuary at St. James's from his inside coat pocket.

"Is this familiar?" he handed the sketch across to Dr. Chapman.

The doctor studied it, then slowly laid it on the desktop. He seemed to be attempting to decide what to say next.

"You must understand, Mr. Brodie, that it was an impression that drew my attention. As I've said, the wounds were horrific, deep, any one could have caused death." His gaze dropped to that sketch.

"There was a mark, quite superficial in comparison, that caught my attention. It looked very much like your sketch. Almost like..."

"Like what, sir?"

"I am not a religious man, Mr. Brodie. Yet when I first saw the mark, it looked very much like a cross that had been made on the young man's chest. Mind you, it was crudely made. But there were no other marks nearby. The other wounds were low in the abdomen.

"I have seen a great many things, Mr. Brodie, in my service with the Queen's army in foreign places, and in my profession. But in that one moment, the thought occurred to me that it was very much as if the murderer had left a deliberate mark."

But what did it mean?

"Considering who you are making inquiries for, I suppose there is no harm in telling you that I've had another visitor regarding the matter," Dr. Chapman added.

"A gentleman by the name of Sir Avery Stanton."

Brodie was not surprised. Stanton was intelligent and persistent, not to mention that he was director of special services to the Queen, charged with investigating certain matters that might pose a threat to the Crown.

"I have worked with Sir Avery in the past," he replied, then retrieved the sketch and tucked it into his coat pocket.

It was true as far as it went, and he left it at that. There was no point in discussing the present situation other than the reason he'd been asked to make inquiries, which he had already provided.

"I thank ye for yer time, sir."

Nor was he surprised when he arrived back at the office on The Strand and Mr. Cavendish informed him that a gentleman by the name of Stanton had called at the office earlier.

"He left this envelope; said that he would return."

Twelve

MIKAELA

LILY AND I returned to the office on The Strand after our visit with the director of White's Gentleman's Club.

"No women allowed," Lily commented.

"Only certain women, for entertainment purposes," I replied.

She drew her own conclusion to that, from her previous experience before coming to London.

"Whores and prostitutes."

"You could say that."

"I did say that," she replied. "Not surprising, it's just a fancier place than the Church." A place where she had been employed as a "ladies' maid", in that previous inquiry where we first met.

"Has Mr. Brodie returned?" I inquired, evading commenting directly about her comment.

Mr. Cavendish nodded. "Just a while ago, and there was a

visit from a gentleman while you were both gone, by the name of Stanton."

It hadn't taken long for Sir Avery to learn we were making inquiries into the death of the son of Lord Salisbery, and now the son of Sir Huntingdon.

I glanced up at the office on the second-floor landing.

"And now?" I inquired. I had no desire to see the man.

"He left a note for Mr. Brodie, then said he would return."

When I would have held the coachman over to take Lily back to Sussex Square, she had disappeared.

"I believe the young miss took the lift," Mr. Cavendish informed me.

I glanced up to see that she had arrived and had entered the office.

I had hoped that she might be satisfied with the day, had decided that the inquiry business was quite boring, and be done with any further interest. It appeared that I was mistaken.

"We learned something that might be important," she was saying quite excitedly as I entered the office.

Brodie glanced up from where he sat, the drawing I'd made before him on the desk, along with a note that he'd obviously just opened. He sat back in his chair.

"Is it important?" she inquired.

I was aware that I suddenly had two choices. I could proceed to explain what we had learned in our visit to White's that included our conversation with the footman from that night when young Salisbery had departed the club.

Or I could let Lily continue, which of course, would naturally encourage her involvement.

I thought of that earlier conversation with Brodie. He was right of course. I couldn't lock her up at Sussex Square to protect her from the outside world. Point of fact, she already knew a great deal more about that "world" from her years at the "Church" in Edinburgh.

The choice was obvious: Pressing the issue despite my feelings on the matter.

"Please continue," I told her. "The information may be helpful."

I must admit that Lily gave an almost perfect account of what we had learned. She didn't embellish but gave a thorough description of our visit, our conversation with the director, and then our additional conversation with the footman who had seen the young man off after he left the club that night.

"It seems that he was quite into the drink and had difficulty making his way to the coach that arrived. The footman had called for a coach, as was his usual responsibility. He thought it odd that it arrived rather quickly," she recounted what he had told us.

"Then, after he assisted the young gentleman aboard, he noticed that the driver stopped at the end of the street and a man stepped out. There was no fog that night, and he was able to see quite clearly.

"He thought it strange that the man did not seem to have any difficulties from having too much to drink, though it did seem as if the man was somewhat impaired with a limp in the left leg. The driver then carried on afterward.

"That is a great deal more than appeared in the police report," Brodie commented. "There was no mention about what happened after the young man left the club."

"Mr. Masterson also shared that the following day was his usual day apart from the club and he has not been questioned by the police. When he inquired with the director of the club, he was told that it was a private matter for Lord Salisbery, and he was not to speak of it among the staff at the club as it would only cause rumor and speculation."

"Ye did well," Brodie complimented Lily. "It is helpful. Ye might add the information to the notes on the chalkboard."

I watched as Lily stepped to the board and took out the small notebook she had carried that morning. She was most serious as she began.

It did seem, as Brodie said, that I had very little choice in the matter, no matter what my concerns for her.

I caught that dark gaze watching me.

"And for yourself?" I inquired. "Were you able to meet with Lord Salisbery's physician?"

"Aye, reluctantly at first on his part until I mentioned that we were inquiring on behalf of His Highness."

I sat on the chair across from his desk. "You learned something important."

"Doctor Chapman was verra thorough in his examination of the wounds. He is a surgeon as well as physician, and it was his opinion that any one of the wounds was sufficient to cause death."

"Yet there were several," I recalled from the notes in the report.

"Aye. To quote the good doctor, it appeared that the wounds were made out of rage, not the sort of thing a thief would take the time for in a robbery." He pushed the sketch across the desk toward me.

"He recognized this. According to what he observed, a mark very near this was made on Salisbery's chest. It wasn't deep and wouldn't have caused his death."

I stared at the sketch. A mark made by the murderer, almost identical to the mark I'd made a sketch of during our visit to St. James's Mortuary.

"He described it as looking like a cross."

"I thought the same when I saw it." Lily had stepped away from the chalkboard and now stood at my shoulder.

"I've seen that sort of thing before," she continued. "At the 'Church', in Edinburgh on the wall of one of the old chambers. According to stories told on the street, the sick and dying were taken there.

"I found it when the 'Church' was all quiet during the daytime, when the girls were asleep and I had finished my chores. I went exploring in the rooms below that had been locked off before Madame set up the 'Church' for business."

I caught Brodie's amused expression and chose to ignore him.

"I took a lantern with me. Some of the cots were still there and I saw marks on the walls beside them. As if the poor souls there had made the sign of the cross as they were dyin'."

It was dreadful to listen to it. She had been quite a bit younger then, and I could only imagine the horror of it.

It perhaps explained her fierceness when she had discovered the sword room at Sussex Square and insisted that I show her how the weapons were used.

Or perhaps it was there in her sudden silences that had eventually grown fewer when she simply chose not to discuss the memory.

It was another glimpse into who Lily was before I brought her to London. It did seem that things we experienced in the past were always part of who we were, no matter the education or care from others, as Brodie had reminded me.

I looked at the sketch again, and then at the one Lily had made that was tacked up on the wall beside the chalkboard.

A cross? If so, what did it mean?

There was more, of course. That envelope and note on the

desk in front of Brodie. It was from Sir Avery Stanton of the Special Services Agency.

"It seems that he has been made aware of the inquiries we have been making. He has requested a meetin'," Brodie explained.

"Will you agree to meet with him?"

"Perhaps, but first we need to meet with His Highness. With what we have now learned it does appear there is more to this than he has shared with us. And now, with the information from the good doctor about young Salisbery's wounds and this..."

He reached across the desk and retrieved the sketch.

"I am not willing to continue until we know all of it."

Pressing the issue, of course, was easier said than done.

He had me write out the brief message he wanted sent to Marlborough House.

I modified the language somewhat. The Prince of Wales was known to have a rather "strong" temperament. Still, it clearly set out that we would not continue the case until His Highness agreed to meet with us.

"It is not a suggestion," Brodie pointed out as he stood over me while reading the note.

"I thought it best to be more diplomatic rather than make a demand. Honey to bees for instance?" I suggested.

He shook his head then departed for the office of the courier service.

"What about bees?" Lily asked after he had left.

It was something Aunt Antonia had once explained to me. However, her version was somewhat different.

"You hear it from time to time; however, I've never believed in it," she told me at the time.

I might have been about the age of ten or twelve, after she had taken Linnie and me to live with her.

I explained the old saying to Lily about bees being attracted to honey rather than vinegar as far as attempting to persuade someone to do something.

"Vinegar is foul and nasty," she agreed. "However, it would bring far quicker results."

I made no comment on that as we added notes to the chalkboard regarding our meeting at White's and Brodie's meeting with Lord Salisbery's physician, most particularly his impression regarding the mark that had also been made on the first victim's body.

Brodie quickly returned from the courier office. He had been assured by the clerk that the message would be delivered straight away once the man saw where it was to be delivered.

A response, from the Prince of Wales, arrived barely more than an hour later, and we prepared to depart for Marlborough House with my notes, and the sketches that Lily and I had made.

"I would like very much to accompany ye," she commented. "I believe that I have contributed adequately with my sketch and information we learned today."

She was correct, of course. She had shown enormous intelligence, poise, and tenacity, as now.

"Of course," I replied.

I could have sworn that little voice inside that made itself known from time to time, suddenly laughed.

It was a silent ride to Marlborough House in that way that

Brodie had of turning things over in his thoughts such as how best to present what we had learned, and then the questions we now had for things the Prince of Wales had not previously shared.

I had retrieved Lily's sketch from the wall of the office and given it to her before we left The Strand. She had tucked it into her bag with a solemn expression that suddenly disappeared at the sight of the uniformed guards and footmen dressed in formal livery as we arrived.

"Crivvens!" she exclaimed. "Do they dress like that every day?"

The coach came to a stop before the main entrance and a footman approached. Lily and I were assisted to alight, then Brodie stepped down as well.

The night of the celebration for the Prince of Wales's birthday, Marlborough House had been overflowing with arrivals, guests already within, dozens of liveried footmen to see to the needs of each guest.

This afternoon was quite different by contrast, although there were still a good many staff and servants going about their duties. Along with those who were there to meet with the Prince of Wales on some matter of official business.

It was no secret that the Queen was the monarch. Yet it was also known in certain circles that the Prince of Wales was kept informed on matters affecting the government, including the military and foreign developments.

We were escorted into the foyer where we were greeted by Sir Knollys.

"If you will be so good as to wait, I will inform His Highness that you have arrived."

He then went to the library where we had previously met with Prince Edward.

A gentleman I recognized emerged from the library with a

leather document case. He briefly nodded in acknowledgement.

"Lady Forsythe."

I replied and explained as he departed.

"He is the Foreign Secretary. We met previously."

He was immediately followed by Sir Knollys's return.

"If you will please follow me."

Prince Edward was cordial in his greeting as we arrived at the library. Then, at a nod, Sir Knollys departed, the door closing behind him.

"You have new information, Mr. Brodie?" His Highness inquired, once again dispensing with any formality.

"Aye," Brodie replied, as Lily and I took seats before the desk. "And questions, sir," he added.

Brodie then explained those we had spoken with, information we had obtained—or not, as in the case of the newspaper archives—and our visit to the St. James's morgue.

"Continue," His Highness said as he stood before the windows, his back turned toward us so that it was impossible for me to know his expression.

"We have additional information from the physician who attended the body of Lord Salisbery's son, and we were able to view the second body from the evening past."

"Go on."

"There is a similarity in two of the wounds."

Prince Edward turned. "Similarity? Might that indicate the same person is responsible?"

"It might verra well." Brodie took out the sketches that Lily and I had made. He laid them at the desk.

"These two sketches were drawn after the incident the other evening. I made this one from my visit with the physician who assisted in the matter of Lord Salisbery's son. He recognized the two drawings. As you can see, the one I made is almost identical."

His Highness approached the desk once more and studied the sketches.

"Lady Forsythe was able to speak with a footman from White's who had not been questioned previously." Brodie continued with a look over at me.

I explained what I had learned about young Salisbery's departure that evening, the coach that had arrived quickly just after Mr. Masterson had called for one, the stop the driver made at the street end not far from the club after departing, and the man seen departing the coach who was not young Salisbery.

"The footman who summoned the coach saw quite clearly as the weather was mild and there was no fog that night," I continued. "He described the man who departed the coach as having an obvious limp of the left leg. The driver then continued on, and the young man's body was discovered when he arrived at his family residence."

His Highness nodded and I continued.

"The man who was seen running from Marlborough House by Miss Montgomery the other evening did have a limp in the left leg.

"There is something more," I added.

Brodie and I had discussed what we would tell His Highness before leaving the office. We agreed that, from what we had learned, it did seem there was information the Prince of Wales had not shared with us. Brodie nodded for me to continue.

"Something that could be important to the case."

Prince Edward nodded. "Please go on, Lady Forsythe."

"The note that was left by the murderer here at Marlborough House had that disturbing message—'*Now there are two.*' It does seem as if there will be more attacks. I learned information when we began our inquiries." I deliberately did not mention that it came from my great aunt. "However, when I attempted to unearth more about it, it seems that great care was taken to remove it from the newspapers."

Brodie had cautioned me about what His Highness's reaction might be to information that my great aunt had provided. Yet, with the reference in notes found on the two bodies, it did seem there could be a connection.

As we had discovered in the past, certain questions often best came from him with his experience as an inspector with the MET and his reputation in private inquiry cases. And of course, there was the very real possibility that when asked, His Highness would simply show us the door and that would be the end of it.

Brodie was respectful of the man who stood across from us. Yet at the same time, he was direct with his next question.

"What can ye tell us, Yer Highness, about the *Four Horsemen of the Apocalypse?*"

Thirteen

I CAUGHT His Highness's reaction, eyes narrowed, lips parted as if he was about to deny any knowledge of the Four Horsemen. Then, he looked down at the desktop, his left hand clenched in a fist, and the frown amid the grey streaked beard that was almost a grimace of pain.

A moment passed, then another. Edward Albert, Prince of Wales, and heir to the throne, sat down heavily in the chair behind the desk.

"Sir Knollys," he called out and his personal secretary appeared as if he had been waiting just beyond that door, which of course, he had.

"You will cancel my next meeting, and I am not to be disturbed until I send for you."

"That would be the meeting with Mr. Gladstone?" his secretary inquired, to make certain of the instructions.

I recognized the name of the prime minister.

"If he has not yet left his office, a reschedule will be necessary. If he arrives, please make my apologies," the Prince of Wales replied. Then repeated, "We are not to be disturbed."

Several moments of silence followed after Sir Knollys left as His Highness appeared to gather himself and consider what he would say in response to Brodie's last question.

"There are matters that might be best spoken of between men," Prince Edward eventually replied. "Perhaps the young lady would like to see the gardens in the solarium."

Perhaps? It was not a suggestion. And while I might have insisted on remaining while Lily toured the gardens, I decided to accompany her.

I was confident that Brodie would ask the questions we had discussed. Still, it was the idea of being set aside, as women often were, that frustrated me, people assuming that we had no brains or the stomach for the deeds of men.

"Of course," I politely replied.

I caught that bemused expression on Brodie's face as Lily and I departed. He had obviously been waiting for me to make a comment that might have been considered inappropriate.

However, I thought our time might be just as useful for something I had in mind.

"Ye let them just send us off!" Lily exclaimed after the library door closed behind us.

"There are times we must pick our battles. This was one of them. Mr. Brodie will provide the details afterward. However..." I added as I glanced about for any among the staff, including Sir Knollys, who might interfere with what I intended.

"Do we wait for Sir Knollys to show us the way to the solarium?" Lily inquired.

The head stablemaster had been questioned after the dreadful incident during the birthday celebration. Yet, I know well enough there were things that might have been overlooked or simply not mentioned. And returning, specifically to inspect the stables, might be hindered by someone watching over my shoulder.

"I believe a visit to the stables could be far more interesting."

"The stables?" Lily replied. "Are we supposed to ask permission?"

"There does not seem to be anyone presently about to ask." I caught her confused expression.

"You do know the way to the stables?"

She smiled and we proceeded toward the solarium, then left Marlborough House by way of the glass doors on the far side that opened out onto the green, with the long row of stables and the coach barn beyond.

The lawn was soggy, my boots sinking in as I gathered up the hem of my skirt and crossed it quickly, arriving at the main stable building where Lily had followed the man that previous night.

"It was just here that I encountered the stablemaster and lost sight of the man as he cut through the hedgerow and disappeared," Lily explained.

"What are we looking for?" she then asked.

"He came this way and then disappeared," I replied. "Look for anything out of the ordinary that might tell us how he accomplished that."

What I hoped we might find by daylight was not within the stables proper but perhaps along the east side that led to that hedgerow and the woods beyond.

I slowly rounded the front of the stables, scanning the ground as we gradually approached the hedgerow behind the stables and coach house.

The gap in the hedgerow was almost indiscernible, yet

there were several branches that had broken away where someone could have passed through.

"How did ye know he would have come this way?" Lily asked.

"It is the only way he might have come without being seen by the guards along the wall." Short of explaining that I'd had my share of escapes in the past, I simply explained that it was very like the forest at Sussex Square.

I pushed through that narrow gap. Branches snagged my hair and skirt as Lily followed. We eventually emerged into the woods behind the hedgerow.

It was filled with deep shadows as light barely reached through the canopy of the trees overhead.

"What do we look for now?" Lily inquired.

She had mud on her skirt. I could only imagine what I might have accumulated breaking through the thick hedge.

"There has to be some place where the man you saw passed through, a path perhaps, more broken branches. Search in that direction." I indicated the direction to the right as I moved to the left.

"No more than twenty paces," I cautioned as we both set off. "He managed to leave quickly, so there should be some indication of the way he passed through."

I scanned the low hanging tree cover and the ground as daylight overhead continued to fade with the late hour. I found nothing.

Was it possible the murderer had escaped in a different direction?

It was then Lily called out. I immediately backtracked and followed the direction she had gone. I found her standing beside a large oak that had shed most of its leaves with the change of the season.

One of the low branches, thin and only a few feet off the ground, had snapped off. Just beyond was another broken branch, as if something or someone had passed into the tree cover.

"Let's see what we can find," I replied as I gathered my skirts in hand and entered the tree cover of oaks and pine.

The forest was thick and dense, and several times our way was blocked. We then found more branches and low scrub that had either been snapped off or pushed back and continued on before coming to a stop once more. We both searched the surrounding tree cover.

"This way, the grasses on the ground appear to have been stepped on," Lily announced.

I nodded and she pushed ahead. We had gone no more than a few paces when I suddenly came up behind her as she stopped. She held something in her hand.

It was a neck scarf. There were no discerning marks to identify it, yet it did not seem to have been there long as it was not muddied or stained, and not what one expected to find deep in the dense cover of trees.

"It could have been lost when His Highness and his companions were last hunting," I told her.

"Or by the man I saw that night?" Lily suggested.

"Perhaps." I carefully folded it and put it in my bag.

We then continued through the tree cover until we reached the high stone wall that surrounded Marlborough House, the grounds, and that forest of trees.

Lily let out a sound of frustration.

"Do ye think the man might have gone over the wall?"

Almost anything was possible, I thought. Still, it would be difficult with the description of the man she had seen fleeing that night with an obvious limp, perhaps from some previous injury, that might have prevented an easy escape.

Or did he possibly have assistance?

"Here!" Lily called out. She had discovered two sets of footprints in the mud on the ground below the wall.

One set was quite large, perhaps from a work boot and deep in the mud. The man wearing it would have been of considerable size.

The second set of prints was somewhat smaller, no doubt made by someone of less height and weight, and one foot seemed to have dragged across the mud.

The man with a limp?

I looked up at the wall. It would have been no difficult task for a taller man of good strength to scale the wall.

An accomplice perhaps who had accompanied the murderer? And then helped him escape?

I took out my notebook and pen.

It was rapidly growing dark as I measured then quickly sketched both sets of footprints that might well not be there after the next rain.

We then made our way back through the forest, that thick hedgerow, and arrived back at the stables as darkness fell.

Lights had come on all along the grounds including the green behind Marlborough House.

One of the house stewards greeted us as we arrived. He looked at us with some alarm, then his expression flattened in that way of royal guards and servants.

Sir Knollys arrived as well.

"Lady Forsythe?"

There were times when a small stretch of the truth was necessary in the scheme of things.

"The solarium is magnificent, Sir Knollys. My compliments to the gardener and his staff," I told him. "We decided to take a stroll about the gardens in the last light. Magnificent. However, we took a wrong turn. Yet here we are."

"In consideration of recent events, Lady Forsythe, it might have been wiser to remain in the solarium where there are those who might provide assistance if you should need it."

That stern gaze took in my somewhat disheveled appearance from trekking about the grounds and forest.

"I appreciate your concern," I replied as the steward we had first encountered stood at attention with a somewhat startled expression at the sight of us. "However, as you can see, we have arrived quite safely." And before he could comment further, "Is Mr. Brodie still with His Highness?"

"They have just concluded. Allow me to escort you to the library," he stiffly replied.

The expression on Brodie's face as we arrived was most entertaining. There was a comment that he chose not to make at our somewhat disheveled appearances. Instead, he nodded to Sir Knollys.

"Thank ye, sir," he said instead and escorted us to the main entrance to the palace.

Our driver had waited at the edge of the courtyard and promptly swung the coach about. Brodie assisted Lily, then myself, into the coach and climbed in after.

"I am almost afraid to ask where the two of ye have been." He handed his handkerchief to me.

"There is mud on yer right cheek."

That might also explain the look from Sir Knollys, I thought.

"We went on a walk," Lily explained.

"A bit of an adventure?" he replied with an amused expression.

She looked over at me as the driver traversed the courtyard and then out onto the driveway and stopped at the gatehouse at the front entrance of the stone wall that surrounded the estate.

"You might have the driver turn to the north," I suggested.

"And that would be for wot reason?" Brodie replied. "Although I am certain there is a very good reason the both of ye look as if ye've just crawled through a hedgerow."

Not far off.

"It is in the matter of the other evening and the possible means by which the murderer managed to escape," I explained.

"Show him the scarf we found," Lily added.

I removed the folded scarf from my bag. While there was only the light from the lantern inside the coach and the street-lamps at both sides of the gatehouse, it was enough for him to discern what it was.

"Where did you find this?"

"Lily found it beyond the hedgerow behind the stables. It had not been there long and might possibly be important."

"Show him the sketches ye made," she added excitedly. "There were footprints in the mud at the far wall just beyond the tree cover behind the stables."

I handed him my notebook. "It does seem as if perhaps another man was present that night who met the attacker there. The man with the limp might have had some difficulty escaping over the wall."

Brodie studied the sketch I'd made, somewhat crude I admit, then leaned out the window of the coach and directed the driver to take the roadway the direction I had suggested.

It was not difficult to find the section of the wall that ran behind the stables and that thick line of trees with branches that hung over the top of the wall that would have no doubt hidden the two men as they fled.

Brodie had the driver stop and stepped down from the coach. Lily and I followed.

She looked at me with a grin, dark eyes gleaming with excitement, as we made our own search of the wall, the sidewalk that ran below it, and the ground with that line of trees, beyond to the roadway.

Brodie found marks on the wall where it appeared that something or someone had scraped the stones, perhaps as they climbed over and then dropped to the sidewalk.

"And two sets of muddied boot marks on the sidewalk just here," he commented.

He then looked past the sidewalk to the space that separated it from the road with the row of trees. He pulled the small handheld lamp he carried and shone the beam across the ground between two trees opposite those two sets of dried prints on the sidewalk.

"More marks here," he pointed out as he crouched down for a closer look.

One set of prints was quite large and deep, the same as those Lily and I had found on the ground on the opposite side of the wall. The second set was not as large with a long mark in the mud as if the other man had dragged his left foot!

Fourteen

AFTER ACCOMPANYING LILY BACK to Sussex Square, we returned to the office on The Strand so that I could add the notes about what Lily and I had discovered to those we already had. And I was most anxious to hear what Brodie had learned from his conversation with His Highness.

"He was reluctant to tell me anythin' at first," Brodie explained as he loosened his tie, then leaned his head against the chair back.

I poured us each a dram of my great aunt's very fine whisky. Perfect on an evening after take-away supper from the Public House, the cold that had set in with the weather, and a fire in the coal stove.

"I can imagine how you were able to persuade him." I handed him a glass. There was a faint smile in one corner of his mouth.

"I mentioned that unusual title that her ladyship recalled from his university days."

"The Four Horsemen."

He nodded. "And explained that ye had discovered that all

mention of it appeared to have been removed from the newspaper archives. I then explained that there might verra well be a connection to the notes that have been left on the bodies of the two young men. And that last note that may indicate that the murderer is not finished."

Most interesting. "What was his response?"

"He didna deny that unusual title."

"And the note with that quote from the Bible?" I inquired.

"*Sins of the fathers.*" He took a sip of whisky.

"It seems there was a particular incident their second year at university that could have meant a serious difficulty for the young prince and his companions."

That did seem to match what my great aunt remembered from about that same time.

"Prince Albert had gone to Cambridge," I recalled what was well known. "And Prince Edward left shortly after and took up a commission in the army. Perhaps to avoid a scandal?" I suggested.

"So it would seem," Brodie replied.

"And the others who were known as the Four Horsemen?" That dark gaze met mine.

"Lord Salisbery and Sir Huntingdon are two of them."

"Who was the fourth member of their private little club?"

"Sir Alfred Walsingham."

Though I was not personally acquainted with him, I still recognized the name. Sir Alfred was a prominent barrister and judge in the royal courts.

"It seems that his son died in a riding accident six months ago in St. James's Park."

That took me a moment. Four young men who became known as the Four Horsemen of the Apocalypse during their time at university. And now, over thirty years later, the sons of three of them were dead?

My thoughts raced.

I did not keep up with the death notices in the newspapers, something I found to be morbid and quite boring. However, what Brodie had learned made sense about that note—*"And then there was one."*

What reason were three young men now dead? I returned to the chalkboard.

"The Four Horsemen"

Did the deaths of three young men have something to do with the reason His Highness was abruptly removed from university years before, and then promptly entered the army and was sent to a distant post?

I stared at the chalkboard.

"The sins of the fathers…" I repeated what had been found in that first note that was discovered. "What sins?"

"I did inquire about that, as well," Brodie commented. "It seems there was a particular incident that occurred and became known to the university. Not the usual sort of college pranks."

"What sort of incident?"

"According to His Highness, he and his companions were celebrating end of term with others at a local inn near the university. There was a great deal of drink and gambling through the night, as might be expected."

The usual sort that young men engaged in, according to my great aunt and other stories I had heard before. Yet, what did that have to do with what was happening now? Excesses like the rumored activities at private gentlemen clubs? What motive was that for murder?

Brodie emptied his glass. "His Highness was adamant that

he doesna know anything more, but there is worry now for his own son."

Arrangements had been made to send the Duke of York and his wife from London for his protection, particularly after the death of his older brother the year before from influenza, as he would one day succeed Prince Edward as regent.

"The sins of the fathers."

"Might there be something to be learned at the college they attended?" I commented. "It might be worth a trip there. I would need to find out who Aunt Antonia knows who might be able to provide information in that regard. I'll inquire in the morning.

"And perhaps there might be something to be learned in speaking with Sir Walsingham," I added regarding that fourth member of that elite, if notorious, young men's club.

"Aye, that could be useful."

We returned to the townhouse even though it was late in the evening.

As Brodie pointed out, after crawling through the hedgerow with Lily, I was in much need of a bath.

The shower compartment that I'd had installed was one of those modern inventions that I thoroughly enjoyed. And it did have other...interesting aspects.

Brodie departed for the office early the next morning. He wanted to learn if the police had made any progress in their investigation into what were now two recent murders, while I wanted to speak with my great aunt.

"Yes, dear, I do know Sir Walsingham, through his wife, of course. Terrible tragedy the accident their son was involved in several months back. She is quite a lovely person, and he was such a bright young man. It must have been devastating for them both.

"The official mourning period is over, and she may be willing to speak with you," she added. "I will put out a telephone call to her. I presume this has something to do with your present inquiry case?"

Very sly the way she worked in a question about our case. I did not go into details about what we had learned, even though she had been present that night at Marlborough House when it appeared that Sir Huntingdon's son was tragically murdered. Nor did I explain my adventures through the hedgerow with Lily.

Instead, I hoped that she might know someone associated with Trinity College who could tell us more about that incident that had happened over thirty years before.

"I shall expect you then," she said after inviting me to join her at Sussex Square.

I called for a cab and quickly dressed.

"Sir Laughton might be able to assist you there," she replied as I inquired about His Highness's time at Cambridge over late morning coffee and biscuits.

"He attended law school at Cambridge. That might have been about the same time as the Prince of Wales, as they are very near the same age."

"Lily was quite excited when she returned yesterday, although she wouldn't reveal what she had been about with you," she commented. "I daresay her clothes were in quite a disarray and badly stained."

She let that dangle, and then, when I did not comment, "Oh, very well, it is obvious that you cannot share matters regarding the situation the other evening at Marlborough House. And the dailies have apparently been 'requested' to print nothing about it other than the brief mention of an 'accident.'

"Accident, my foot!" she exclaimed. Then, when I offered no comment, "Very well, since you will not discuss the matter, I will have to learn the details elsewhere."

Which of course, would be the latest gossip among her "ladies," those distinguished members of her card group, some of whom no doubt had attended as well.

It would have been far simpler if they gathered for a few games of whist, or a seance with Madame Sybille.

Not one to throw cold water on the woman's talent, she had provided some very interesting information in other situations. Still, Brodie was not inclined to put much weight in her abilities.

"And always for a sizeable fee from her ladyship," he had commented in the past. "Ye surprise me that ye would even consider the woman's advice."

I did not admit that I had reluctantly participated in one of my great aunt's gatherings, as she called them.

During that session, Madame had proceeded to read my cards and had predicted new adventures that I would be taking along with a dark-eyed stranger. This was just after my return from the Greek Islands where Brodie had retrieved me from certain ruin and scandal.

It did seem as if Madame had some insight into certain things.

I could only hope that whatever my great aunt was able to learn from her "source," as she referred to Madame, that she would not then take herself off on her own inquiries as she had once declared. I remembered the conversation quite well.

"We could start our own investigations. It could be quite exciting! I would imagine that it could reveal just who is sleeping with whom among the ton. And then there is always a murder or two thrown into the mix."

As I was saying…I knew Sir Laughton, my aunt's lawyer, quite well and telephoned his office from Sussex Square. He was not due in court and agreed to meet with me at his office near the Crown Courts.

"Mr. Hastings is available to take you to his office," Aunt Antonia insisted. "The weather seems to have taken a nasty turn this morning,"

Not that I was fooled. She could be quite clever, and no doubt hoped to learn something from her coachman when he returned.

"There are all sorts of persons around the courts. It might be best if I accompany ye," Munro commented when he arrived to announce that Mr. Hastings had arrived at the porte cochère at the entrance to the manor.

I suppose that I should have been surprised to find Lily in the coach. I was not.

"I can make notes for ye," she informed me.

It did seem as if she had overheard my conversation with Aunt Antonia.

It was a paltry excuse at best as I was quite capable of making my own notes. Yet, Brodie's earlier comment was there —that I could support her participation or attempt to thwart it, in which case she would go about it in her own way.

Case in point the previous evening at Marlborough House, when she had discovered the means by which it seemed the murderer and another man had escaped.

"Very well," I agreed. "But then you will immediately return here."

"Of course," she replied, in a manner that was not at all convincing.

I caught the frown on her face as her gaze slipped past me to Munro, who intended to accompany us to Sir Laughton's office at the law courts.

"An escort?" she pointedly inquired.

It was not the first time I had noticed that there did seem to be some difficulty between the two of them. Lily's expression was quite obvious.

"It will not be necessary for you to accompany us," I told him as he assisted me into the coach.

"Mr. Hastings is quite adept at navigating London traffic, and I am quite well armed," I assured him.

"Verra well," he snapped obviously not pleased as he stood back from the coach, and we departed.

"I canna go anywhere without him accompanying me," Lily shared. "As if I need a chaperone. Bloody stubborn Scot!"

With the rain that had turned to icy snow and clogged the streets, it was a slow trip across the city and very near midday by the time we arrived at Sir Laughton's office.

"Miss Montgomery as well," he acknowledged Lily. "Always a pleasure. And the weather has not put you off, I see," he said by way of greeting as we were shown to his private office within the large office occupied by two of his law clerks.

"Not at all," I replied as we handed over our coats and umbrellas to one of them.

"And somewhat urgent according to Lady Antonia, which could only mean that it is a matter of some importance," he surmised and thanked the clerk, not speaking again until he had gone.

"Lady Montgomery did convey that I am to assist in whatever way I can. A new inquiry case, Lady Forsythe? Perhaps that dreadful business at Marlborough House?"

He had obviously spoken to Aunt Antonia after we departed Sussex Square. He waited as his clerk returned with hot coffee, then sat back in his high-backed chair after the young man left.

"How may I help?"

Lily took out her notebook and pen as I explained.

"You attended law school at Cambridge at about the same time as His Highness."

He nodded, fingers steepled before him, a thoughtful expression on his face. "Yes, my first years there."

"Were you aware of the situation when His Highness departed somewhat abruptly?"

"A long time ago. I presume this has to do with the accident at Marlborough House."

"We have been asked to make inquiries," I replied.

"I see. You realize that I must remain discreet for all sorts of reasons."

"I understand, still there may be something that you remember about an incident that occurred then, and a particular title four students including the Prince of Wales were known as."

That thoughtful gaze sharpened. "A long time ago, there were the usual sort of university mischiefs by young men from time to time."

"What can you tell us about the Four Horsemen and His Highness's abrupt departure."

"You are particularly well informed," he replied. "That has

not been spoken of in more than thirty years." He rose from his chair and paced about the office as he seemed to consider what to tell us.

"Membership was exclusive to just four members. There was speculation about certain activities that went on. The usual sort, drinking, carousing, and hunting adventures around the local countryside. And an incident as you called it at the end of the term.

"All four of the young gentlemen were called to the office of the dean of Trinity College, as well as their families.

"There were rumors that they might be expelled, along with gossip from the village nearby," he added. "His Highness departed almost immediately after the arrival of Prince Edward. The other three students involved in the matter were severely reprimanded and forbidden to go into the village. However, they were allowed to remain at university."

"Who might know the details of the situation that led to his sudden departure?"

"The Master of Trinity College, no doubt, who was compelled to notify the royal family. That would have been Master Whewell."

He shared that he knew William Whewell had passed on only a handful of years after the "incident" that had caused such a stir.

"Might anyone else have known about it?" I then asked.

"It is possible the vice chancellor of the college would have known the details, as he would have been required to notify the chairman of the Board of Regents regarding the departure of the Prince of Wales. Not an everyday occurrence and most certainly a situation that might have far-reaching consequences for the university.

"The vice chancellor at the time was Sir Edwin Lowery, who also taught at the law college then.

"He retired several years ago and is no longer with the college. However, he might be able to provide information. I do speak with him on some matters of the law." He then added with candor, "He has a sharp mind and has not forgotten when I was called to his office for reprimand."

Sir Lowery lived in Belgravia, south of Hyde Park, and was held in high esteem. He was frequently called upon and still debated law with those who had studied at Cambridge.

"I presume you would care to call on him in the matter," he said then. "I will have my clerk draw up a letter of introduction. And I will send round a message to inform him that you will be calling on him, although it is not certain that he will be willing to share any details from that long ago."

Fifteen

MR. HASTINGS DELIVERED us to the office on The Strand after we departed our meeting with Sir Laughton.

I was eager to share what we had learned with Brodie, while Lily was not at all eager to return to Sussex Square.

"The Four Horsemen," she commented. "His Highness was the fourth member of the club at university."

And we were no closer to learning who was behind the murders than when we started.

There was another person I wanted to speak with, Lady Walsingham, an acquaintance of Aunt Antonia, regarding the tragic death of her son in that riding accident. Was there a connection?

Mr. Cavendish emerged from the alcove and met us at the sidewalk. The hound appeared to have returned as the weather had worsened, covered with the usual mud and debris from the street, which he decided to share as he loped toward Lily with a toothsome grin.

"Mr. Brodie returned a short while ago," Mr. Cavendish informed us.

"He was to meet with Mr. Dooley." I wanted very much to know what the police had learned from their inquiries into the death of Lord Salisbery's son after he left White's that night.

Mr. Cavendish nodded. "And there was a gentleman waiting for him across the way, though no gentleman in my book. Sir Avery Stanton."

He gave me a long look from under the bill of his cap.

"Gave a taste of his boot to the hound. They came to a rather quick agreement in that regard."

I could well imagine that, as the hound could be quite formidable when provoked. "He seems not to have been injured."

Mr. Cavendish grinned. "Not at all."

I looked at the office on the landing. We knew that Sir Avery, with the Special Services Agency, had been called upon by the Queen regarding the incident at Marlborough House.

He had his sources and could be quite thorough, as I had learned. I was not at all pleased that he was there.

"Sir Avery?" Lily commented, as she gave Rupert strokes about the ears. She was most fond of him. As she had once said, they were both orphans. "What does he want?"

Precisely, I thought.

After a somewhat difficult business in the past where Brodie could have been brought up on charges and imprisoned, he regarded the man with caution and chose not to involve us in any "Crown situations" as they were called.

As for myself, it was quite simple. He was the Queen's man who had been given a great deal of power when it came to protecting the "interests of the Crown" that might fall outside the usual boundaries of propriety or the law.

He felt that he could do almost anything to achieve his own

purposes. To say that I was not fond of the man was a mild understatement. Quite simply, I didn't like or trust the man.

And now, I could only assume that he wanted something from us, information no doubt. Most interesting.

Lily and I proceeded toward the lift. When the hound would have followed, Mr. Cavendish started to call him back.

"It's quite all right," I assured him. "I'm certain a warm fire would be welcome on a day such as this." Not to mention that it would be interesting to see the reaction from Sir Avery.

He grinned. "Miss Effie said as how it was good and warm at the Public House as well. I believe I do hear a pint calling me name—to warm my bones in this weather. What's left of them, that is."

He was not the least impaired after the loss of both legs at the knees in an accident. He wheeled his platform sharply about and launched himself across the roadway in the direction of the Public House, icy rain exploding in clouds around him.

I called Rupert, and we went to the lift and made the slow trip up to the second-floor landing. We arrived just down from the office where a light shone through the glass panes in the door and I could see Sir Avery seated across from Brodie who sat at his desk.

Rupert had run ahead as I opened the gate of the lift. He waited expectantly at the door, ears perked, tail standing up as well in anticipation.

"Should we leave him outside?" Lily inquired. "He is a bit soggy." She wrinkled her nose. "And after that confrontation Mr. Cavendish mentioned."

"Not at all," I replied and opened the door.

Rupert bounded into the warm office. He slid to a stop on the wood floor, in that way I had seen my father's hounds do as a child when they picked up a scent on the hunt. The hound then launched himself.

Sir Avery came part way out of his chair as Rupert attacked.

The instinct to protect himself was wasted as the chair went over backwards with Sir Avery and Rupert amid much snarling and snapping.

Brodie had come out of his chair as well.

The look he gave me was most interesting as he rounded the desk as though to come to Sir Avery's aid amid a good number of curses.

Oh my, I thought. Whoever would have thought this might happen?

"You might want to call him off," Brodie strongly suggested as Lily broke out laughing at the conflagration at the office floor.

Or not?

Still, I suppose it might be considered a serious attack on someone of importance—at least in his own mind.

And more to consider, I did not want some punishment to come down on Rupert, who had come to my aid more than once. Not to mention that I was very fond of him. Particularly at moments like this.

I called him back. Eventually he let go of Sir Avery's pant leg, then came and sat at my feet.

"I have no idea what got into him," I commented as Brodie assisted Sir Avery to his feet.

"He is usually quite docile, though he is fond of food," I added pointedly as Sir Avery inspected himself for any wounds. "Did you perhaps have luncheon before arriving?"

There are times when one's station, family connections,

and even greater wealth than that of the Queen—my great aunt's—could be advantageous.

And although I have never been one to flaunt any of it, I did take particular pleasure in the expression on Sir Avery's face. He was, as Aunt Antonia would have described, quite white around the mouth as he sputtered and cursed.

Lily went into the adjacent room and returned with a towel. She proceeded to wipe mud and debris from Rupert's coat.

"He doesn't seem to be injured," she announced.

"Injured?" Sir Avery roared, quite indignant.

"Another towel might be called for," I suggested, though I didn't give a fig if the man was injured and bleeding.

She brought another towel from the room and handed it to him, with an innocent expression.

"I do hope you are not badly injured, sir."

There was a tear in the sleeve of his coat, and he was quite disheveled. Although, he appeared otherwise unharmed except perhaps a few bruises that would appear later.

Good dog, I thought.

I would have a warm meal brought for him from the Public House for his reward. Mr. Cavendish would be highly disappointed to have missed this second encounter.

Sir Avery straightened his clothes and smoothed a hand back through his hair. He seized his long coat from the coat stand and fumbled as he struggled to pull it on.

"I expect you to be forthcoming in the matter, Brodie," he said then. "I know you well, and I refuse to believe that you have no information in the matter," he snapped.

I glanced at the chalkboard where I had made notes about our progress so far in the case. The board had been wiped clean!

It did seem that Brodie had removed my notes.

Brodie briefly met my gaze as he went to assist Sir Avery with his coat.

"The lift is at the end of the hallway," he informed him. "The stairs can be treacherous in this sort of weather."

No sooner had the door snapped shut behind him and he made his way to lift, than Lily burst out laughing.

Brodie turned to me. "Did it occur to ye that it might have been unwise to let the hound accompany ye? Ye know well enough what the man is capable of. It's usually best not to poke the bear. Although," the smile was there, "it was most entertainin'."

I crossed the office and knelt in front of the hound and rubbed his ears. He licked my hand and grinned.

"For a *bear*,'" I replied. "Sir Avery screamed like a fish monger at market."

"You've erased Mikaela's notes?" Lily commented as she sat on the chair that Sir Avery had occupied before he was attacked.

"In the best interests of our client," Brodie replied. "There was just enough time after Mr. Cavendish announced his arrival."

"It must have been a most interesting conversation," I commented. "Did he share what he has learned about the incident at Marlborough House?"

"It appears that he is not aware of the possible connection to the riding accident at Hyde Park this past April. Or if he was, he did not share it with me."

"Of course not." I didn't bother to hide my sarcasm. "Was he able to provide any insights from his own inquiries on behalf of the Queen?"

The answer was, not surprisingly, "*no*."

"There was the not-subtle reminder I might find it advantageous to make certain that he is informed of anything we learn. It was just about that time that you arrived."

"Advantageous in what way?" I inquired with no small amount of suspicion.

"The advantage of working with the Agency in the future."

We shared a look. I came out of my own chair.

"Bloody hell! The man is a snake. He would sell his mother if he thought it would gain him anything."

"Tell me, wot ye really think of the man," Brodie replied.

I didn't dignify that with a response.

"What else were you able to learn from the conversation?" I then inquired, knowing how very persuasive he could be when he wanted information.

"I did happen to mention the similarity of the marks on the two bodies. He was unaware of them."

"And what of the 'Four Horsemen?'"

"I made no mention of it. He may not have been informed of that, if in fact the Queen was even aware of that private club of theirs before His Highness was removed over that incident."

"What of your meeting with Mr. Dooley?" I inquired as Lily poured coffee for all of us against the cold in the office in spite of the fire in the coal stove.

"It seems there was another potential witness the night young Salisbery was murdered, a woman who is part of the cleaning staff.

"She works the late hours after most of the members and the entertainment for the evenin' have departed.

"Dooley provided her address near the Garden, and I was able to speak with her. She had hired a cab that night to take her and another one of the women to the club as the weather took a turn.

"When they arrived on the side street, down the street from the club, she saw a man make his way to a coach, one of the hired drivers that are near the park. He had a limp in one leg."

"Did she see him clearly?"

"She described him as perhaps no more than thirty years old or so, with fair hair." Brodie paused. "More than that she couldna see. The driver set off and pulled round the corner and stopped."

A driver who waited for the son of Lord Salisbery to leave.

We spent the rest of the afternoon retrieving the notes I'd made from my notebook while Lily typed them on the portable typewriter, adding what we had learned that day as well as what Brodie had learned from the woman who worked at White's.

Mr. Cavendish returned to make certain Rupert hadn't experienced any further "indignity" as he put it. Well aware of our habit of staying over at the office when on a case, he brought food cartons for supper.

"And to make certain Mr. Brodie hadn't pitched his guest into the street. Gettin' rid of a body is always a tricky proposition. Although there is always the river," he suggested. "I know people."

I did not question that.

Before the accident that had taken his legs, he had spent years aboard a merchantman. It was not the first time he mentioned pitching someone overboard.

"And I see the hound is no worse for the experience."

"Ye should have been here," Lily chimed in. "He was magnificent. Sir Avery will have more than a few bruises."

"Good lad," he replied, then spun about and headed for the lift.

"I'll be at the Public House," he called out as he entered the lift. "It's cold out tonight."

No explanation needed there.

After sharing supper, I telephoned my great aunt to let her know that Lily would be staying with us, then returning to Sussex Square in the morning.

"So good of you to let me know," she exclaimed through the earpiece.

She did hate the thing and much preferred an embossed formal note sent round—possible evidence she had once commented, should it be needed.

She hadn't provided details of that and I didn't ask. However, with true Montgomery fortitude, she used the *"damned thing"* as she called the telephone.

She then went on to tell me that she had spoken with Lady Walsingham whose son had died in that riding accident and the grieving mother would be expecting me to call on her.

"I have asked Madame to inquire with her sources in the matter as well," she added. "No stone unturned."

Oh my.

"Who the devil is Madame?" Brodie asked when I explained that I would be meeting with Althea Walsingham after ending the conversation.

I had not previously spoken of Madame Sybille, as I knew Brodie's thoughts regarding such things.

"She is the lady who speaks to spirits," Lily explained. "She has been to Sussex Square several times."

"Speaks to spirits?" Brodie commented as he set more coal in the box of the stove. "Is she perhaps acquainted with Miss Templeton?"

It was not that he didn't think it was possible. I had to admit that my good friend, Templeton, who was currently off on tour with her latest play, was a trifle eccentric. Yet, then, many people considered Aunt Antonia to be eccentric. Precisely what she let them believe.

As she had once explained it to my sister and me, people were often very accommodating, and one could get away with a great deal if they thought one was eccentric or a bit off as she put it. I had seen her use that to her advantage more than once. And it was possible the same was true of my friend.

"You have to admit," I told Brodie, "Templeton has provided information in the past that we might not have learned otherwise."

Lily smiled as Brodie slammed the iron door shut on the stove.

Sixteen

I SET the telephone earpiece back in the cradle. It was early in the morning, yet Althea Walsingham had responded to my note.

Her husband had left for his office at the Exchange for the day, and she had just sent her housekeeper off to the market in spite of the rain. She had been expecting a telephone call from me.

We spoke briefly. I heard the way her voice softly caught as she spoke of her son, then the way she took a breath and then carried on, speaking of the time after the horseback riding accident at Hyde Park.

Aunt Antonia had spoken of her strength in the aftermath. She truly admired her, and my great aunt rarely admired other persons.

I could count them all on one hand. Others were simply wastrels—a somewhat antiquated term—or in her own words, those with feathers for brains.

Never one to mince words, she'd declared, "You live long enough, travel enough, and you realize there are few truly intelligent and good people in the world. Most others are simply cluttering the place up."

I had seen some of that as well in the cases Brodie and I took, where good people were made to suffer for others.

I had several questions to ask Lady Walsingham, yet I was very aware it might become difficult to now learn that—what they believed had been an accident—might very well have been no accident at all.

Lily had folded the comforter she had used the night before. She had slept on the settee in the main office with Rupert on the floor beside her, even though Brodie had offered our bed for Lily and I to share.

He had been perfectly willing to take the settee for the night or the chair at his desk, which he pointed out he had slept in more than once when working late on a case.

"The settee's better than a pub or cold alley. I know how it is between a man and woman," Lily reminded us.

"Aye, we'll make up for it later," Brodie had replied with a wink at her, while I chose to ignore the both of them.

The weather seemed to have settled somewhat during the night. It was not raining at the moment, although ice covered the walkway on the landing and hung from the railing on the second floor. Beyond the sidewalk, The Strand was a sea of slush as morning traffic of wagons and coaches cut paths around delivery carts and coal wagons.

"I'd like to accompany ye," Lily commented as she handed me the folded comforter. "I can make notes."

She had smoothed the wrinkles from her gown, combed her dark hair then tied it back, and made use of tooth powder at the washstand in our bedroom, as it was far too cold to venture down the hall, not to mention risk the icy landing.

"I know everything ye've learned from reading yer notes last night," she added. "And I did assist yesterday at Marlborough House, when ye might not have learned how the murderer escaped."

"It could be useful," Brodie commented. "As ye well know, I've not the fine penmanship that she has. And I'm off to Bond Street to speak with a tailor who might be able to tell us what they can about this."

He held aloft the neck scarf Lily had found in the forest at Marlborough House the day before.

He pulled on his long coat, then took my hand and pulled me close. He brushed my cheek with the back of his fingers.

"And wot of the two of ye?"

It did seem there was no argument there about Lily accompanying me.

"Sir Laughton is to arrange a meeting with the man who was vice chancellor of Trinity College when His Highness and the others attended," Lily announced.

"He may know something of the event that sent Prince Albert to the university just before the Prince of Wales departed," I added. "And we will be meeting with Lady Walsingham," I added. "I telephoned the residence yesterday, and she is willing to meet with us."

"In the matter of the young man who died in that riding accident. It could be important." He nodded, then kissed me.

"Then I will see ye both here afterward."

It did seem as if Lily and Brodie might be forming a campaign against me.

Parry, shift, thrust, and point, well made from her lessons when I had instructed her in the sword room at Sussex Square.

She had learned her lessons well, and I agreed that she could accompany me this morning. I then hoped to meet with the former vice chancellor from Trinity College whom Mr. Laughton had agreed to contact.

Sir John and Lady Walsingham, lived near Highgrove, an area of stately homes and estates. According to Aunt Antonia, the townhouse at number 12 Linden Place was their London residence, with their country home in Surrey which Althea Walsingham had inherited through her family.

They had returned to London at the end of September as the heat lessened in the city and the holiday season approached. The forthcoming Christmas holiday was their first since the death of their son.

There was the usual congestion of traffic on The Strand, particularly as the weather had settled somewhat and people took advantage to tend to their usual tasks at banks, shops, and the marketplace.

Mr. Cavendish was finally able to wave down a coach, the driver, Mr. Jarvis, familiar from previous adventures across the city. He tipped his cap.

"Mornin' ladies, where will it be this fine mornin'?"

It was as I provided him the address at Linden Place that I caught sight of a man who stood head and shoulders above those around him who crowded the sidewalk across The Strand.

It was a fleeting glimpse and then he was gone. Still...

"That be in Highgrove," Mr. Jarvis commented, drawing me back to the moment.

I nodded. "Yes." And climbed into the coach.

"What is it?" Lily had climbed in after me and took the seat across.

I shook my head, not at all certain I had seen anything of importance.

"Nothing," I replied as we settled ourselves for the ride across the city.

Yet I was unable to shake the feeling, more the certainty, that the man I had seen was somehow familiar.

We arrived at the Walsingham residence, and I asked Mr. Jarvis to wait. It was quite possible that the meeting might be very short indeed as I had no way of knowing what to expect when I explained the reason for our visit.

A housemaid answered the door, and I introduced the two of us. She nodded and showed us into the front parlor.

"Her ladyship will be with you presently."

While we waited, I took in the details of the front parlor— the Queen Anne furnishings, two portraits of an older man and woman, perhaps the parents of either Sir Walsingham or Lady Walsingham.

There was a side table beneath windows that looked out onto a narrow garden that separated the Walsingham residence from the next one over. More photographs sat at the table.

One was in sepia tones, the subject was a small child of perhaps three or four years. Another was a tall youth in a school uniform with a shock of dark hair that spilled over his forehead. The last photograph, in black and white tones, was of the same young man with a long rifle and a pair of dead grouse at his feet.

"Our son, Jack. He was named for my husband."

I turned. Lady Walsingham stood framed in the doorway to the parlor.

"We have never met," she said as she came into the room.

"But I have heard of your adventures from Lady Antonia. And now you are here, Lady Forsythe. And the matter you spoke of —I might have hoped for a different occasion to meet."

She had asked the reason I wanted to meet in our brief conversation the day before. I had not gone into detail, only that it was a matter that might be related to her son's accident. Meeting her now, I felt a twinge of regret that it was under such difficult circumstances.

She was an attractive woman, not a great deal older than myself, I would have guessed, with dark brown hair, blue eyes framed by dark lashes, and a soft smile framed by perhaps more lines than she might have had before the accident.

It was there in her eyes as well, a look that I had seen before, that came from the pain of loss and never went away.

"And you are?" she inquired with a look at Lily who introduced herself.

"Ah, Miss Montgomery. Lady Antonia has spoken of you. Perhaps following in Lady Mikaela's footsteps?"

Lily nodded but made no comment.

Lady Walsingham then gestured to the chairs that sat before the fire at the hearth. When the maid reappeared, she ordered tea to be served.

"You spoke yesterday of a matter that might be related to my son's accident."

I waited until tea had been served and the maid then left.

"We have taken an inquiry case that has been most baffling," I began and left out the details of the deaths of the two other two young men.

"There is reason to believe that it may be regarding Sir Walsingham's friendship at university with three young men." I saw the surprise in that soft blue gaze.

"In what way?"

"We've been asked to investigate a recent situation, the attack on a young man at Marlborough House."

She nodded. "Dreadful situation. We did not attend as we have not yet accepted any social invitations. Yet, we were aware of it through others who were there that night. And my husband is acquainted with Lord Huntingdon."

"A gentleman called upon us yesterday, without a previous announcement," she continued. "Sir Avery Stanton of the Special Services. Neither of us were here at the time."

Bloody hell.

I could only imagine what that might have been like if he had been able to question either of them about their son's "accident." Sir Avery had served a career in the military. His manner was blunt and quite brash with little regard for anyone else.

"He left his card with our housekeeper and informed her that he would return. And now you are making inquiries," she added. "It would seem there is more to the situation than our friends were aware of at the time." She folded her hands. "Please speak plainly, Lady Forsythe."

"A man was seen fleeing Marlborough House immediately after young Huntingdon's fall. It is possible that the young man's death was not an accident."

"I see. A situation that might usually be handled by the Metropolitan Police," she commented. "Yet, the Special Services have been called upon, and now questions about Jack's accident."

Grieving, yet with a quiet strength that I admired.

"If it is not too painful, I would like to ask some questions about the day of the accident."

There was a faint, sad smile. "Of course. Although I don't know what I can tell you. He had taken himself off to the stables. He did so like to ride, at our country estate as well. It was in May, a lovely day." She seemed to gather herself.

"We were told the park was quite crowded, as was to be expected, with carriages and other riders about." She paused.

"Sir John, my husband, received word. With so many about in the park, we were told that it appeared his horse had been startled and then bolted. The animal was quite high-strung, although Jack had always handled him well. When others arrived afterward..." She paused once more before continuing. "Jack had been thrown, and there was nothing anyone could do."

"Were there any witnesses to the accident?"

Lady Althea shook her head. "Apparently it all happened very quickly. The constables who were in the park that day apparently questioned several people, but it appears that no one saw anything that might have caused it, other than one man who was seen with Jack before the constables arrived."

"Someone who rode with him that day?"

She shook her head. "He rode alone that day."

"Was the man questioned?"

She shook her head again. "He was gone by the time the constables arrived. It would seem that is not much help for your inquiry case. I apologize that I cannot provide more."

"I know this may be difficult, but I must ask," I then said. "Was there any blood on your son's body, perhaps from a wound during the fall?"

"My husband didn't mention any wound. You see, Jack's neck was broken in the fall," her voice broke softly.

I reached out and laid my hand over hers.

"I am so very sorry."

"It's quite all right. Perhaps a wound might have made more sense. He seemed to simply be sleeping when he was brought here afterward." She was thoughtful,

"His father wanted him to wear a formal set of clothes for mourning, while I felt it was so like him to have been out riding that he should be wearing his riding costume. I suppose it was a foolish thing to have a disagreement over."

"You have his coat from that day?" She had obviously lost the argument.

She looked up. "As I said, it undoubtedly seems foolish."

"Not at all," I replied, then inquired. "Might I see it?"

I fully expected her to refuse.

"Of course." Lady Althea asked her maid to refresh our tea as she went to retrieve her son's riding jacket from that day.

"Do ye believe it might provide a clue?" Lily whispered.

I didn't know what to think. I hated asking it of Lady Walsingham. It was obvious that she had deeply loved her son and to now have inquiries being made about the accident seemed cruel.

Lady Althea returned with several items of clothing over her arm. "I've brought the shirt and pants as well. There are the usual stains on his breeches that one might expect, although I don't know what that might tell you."

She laid the clothes that included buckskin breeches, a vest, dark wool jacket, and shirt with a dark blue cravat on the settee.

There were green stains on the buckskin breeches, not unexpected considering the fall the young man had taken. There was what appeared to be a mud stain on the elbow of the jacket, but no other stains or marks, nor on the shirt, at first glance.

I ran my fingers over the fine silk of the shirt. There was no stain, however, it did appear that something sharp had snagged the silk fabric and left broken threads across the front.

Possibly from a sharp object?

Was it possible someone—perhaps the man who was seen with her son after the accident, had made that mark and had then left as a crowd gathered?

"What is it?" she asked.

"I know this may be very difficult to answer," I replied. "Did Sir Walsingham mention any marks that might have been made?"

Lady Althea looked down at her clenched hands. "My husband saw Jack afterward. He spoke of marks on his chest, though there was no blood from a wound."

"Did he describe what the marks looked like?"

"There were two marks, as I remember what he said at the time. Possibly made by a tree branch during the fall."

Or made after the fall, I thought.

"Was anything found in your son's possession? An envelope or note?"

She shook her head. "As I said, his father saw to everything."

The expression on her face revealed a great deal. Grief that was still raw, but something else. Strength, that slipped past the sadness and grief.

"Why do you ask?"

Again, I chose my words with great care.

"It is possible your son's death was not an accident and may, in fact, be related to the incident at Marlborough House."

I watched her for any sign that what I had just shared with her might be overwhelming, as it would be for most anyone.

I laid my hand over hers once more. "I apologize for any pain our visit has caused. Thank you for meeting with us."

She followed us to the door. "They were known as the Four Horsemen while at University," she said.

I had not expected that she would know about that—the follies of young men—gambling, women for the night, a brotherhood sworn to secrecy.

"Yes, Lady Montgomery spoke of it," she added.

"A dreadful title of their club that included Lord Salisbery and Sir Huntingdon."

I thanked her again for meeting with us.

"You must let me know what you learn," she said in parting.

I promised that I would. It was the least we could do.

"There was something about that young man's riding costume," Lily said as we returned across London. "I saw it on your face."

"There were broken threads on the front of his shirt." And the rest of it?

I thought how best to describe something I wasn't even certain of.

"That mark could have been made by a branch from a nearby tree as the young man fell," she replied.

"Perhaps."

Seventeen

I HAD THOUGHT of taking Lily back to Sussex Square after the meeting with Lady Walsingham.

However, there was only enough time to purchase a sandwich from a vendor, then continue to the meeting Sir Laughton had arranged with the former vice chancellor of Trinity College Cambridge at the time of that incident at the university.

Sir Lowery lived in Belgravia, an area of white stucco residences and townhouses to the east of Kensington. Afternoon street traffic was considerably less as we passed through Knightsbridge and arrived in a timely manner.

From what Sir Laughton had said, Sir Lowery lived in Belgravia with his wife, lecturing at the different colleges, and consulting as a Professor of Law Emeritus.

The housekeeper showed us into the library after we arrived.

Sir Lowery, with a warm brown gaze and a full beard, rose from his desk to greet us.

We exchanged the usual pleasantries, along with my introduction of Lily.

"I must say, Lady Forsythe, that I am an admirer of Emma Fortescue. Quite a remarkable woman. Reminds me of my dear wife, never a dull moment, keeps me on my toes to be certain. She introduced me to your first book.

"Now," he said. "What manner might a college professor be of assistance? A question about law in your inquiry cases perhaps?"

His housekeeper appeared, followed by a small, robust woman with silvered hair. Lady Letitia Lowery, with an apron over her gown and smudges across one cheek.

"Forgive my appearance. I am transplanting day lilies, I don't trust them to anyone else," she said. "Yet, I wanted very much to meet you when Sir Lowery mentioned you would be calling today.

"That young woman—*Emma*, such a wonderful character. Brave, and much her own woman, that whole episode on the Greek Island, so exciting, and that mysterious man at the end!"

"My dear, Lady Forsythe is not here to discuss Greek adventures or her writing endeavors."

She made a gesture with a smudged hand, as if to wave off the criticism. She was not the least intimidated or content to be "put in her place" as some women might have been.

"I do suppose that it is too early in the day for a dram," Lady Lowery commented with that reference to my protagonist, Emma Fortescue.

"Coffee will be fine, Letitia."

"Of course," she beamed and sent their housekeeper off to bring it to the library.

"I must get back to my garden, it has become quite overgrown. I am thinking of adding narcissus and possibly crocus for next spring. The colors will be quite lovely." She paused at the entrance to the library.

"I do hope there will be new adventures for Emma Fortescue, and perhaps more about that mysterious man." She smiled and left without waiting for my response so that we might continue our conversation.

"You must forgive her boldness." Sir Lowery started to apologize.

"Not at all," I assured him. "She is quite wonderful."

He smiled. "Narcissus and crocus. We shall see. Now, how may I assist you in this matter that Sir Laughton spoke of?"

I didn't know how much detail to provide and so decided to begin with that notorious title four young university students had adopted thirty years before while at Trinity College.

"Tell me about the Four Horsemen of the Apocalypse."

"An intriguing request on a subject not many know of." Sir Lowery reached across his desk and picked up his pipe.

"Do you mind, Lady Forsythe?" he inquired.

"Not at all."

Brodie smoked a pipe from time to time, most usually when he was deep in thought over a case, and I enjoyed the fragrance of it.

And very much the same, there was a thoughtful expression on Sir Lowery's face as he scooped tobacco from a humidor on the desk into the bowl of the pipe, tamped it down, then struck a match and lit it.

He squinted slightly, eyeing me thoughtfully through a swirling cloud of fragrant smoke as he puffed away, then put out the match in the small ash pan on the desk.

"The Four Horsemen of the Apocalypse. Revelations, in the New Testament as I remember from my early lessons as a boy," he commented as he continued to study me through that haze of smoke. "Not the usual reading material one expects of an enlightened young woman."

"Nor perhaps that of four young university students," I replied.

He continued to puff away as he watched me.

"Sir Laughton did say that you were most inquisitive," he eventually replied, then seemed to arrive at a decision regarding my visit.

"That was a long time ago."

"Over thirty years," I acknowledged. "When certain things might be forgotten. Yet, it seems that someone has not. What can you tell me about an incident that caused the Prince of Wales to suddenly withdraw from the university thirty-two years ago?"

I was prepared for the usual response—young college men caught in the usual pranks one hears. I hoped for more and waited.

Sir Lowery set his pipe in the ash pan then sat back in his chair.

"You are quite direct, Lady Forsythe."

It was true that I had no patience for innuendoes or polite excuses. Three young men were dead, possibly murdered, sons of three of those four students now grown men in various positions of government and society.

"You seem to have knowledge that, for some, might best be forgotten. The Four Horsemen, brash, headstrong, foolish perhaps.

"I remember it well from my position as vice chancellor under Sir William who was master of Trinity College during that time." He shook his head.

"There was a tragic episode that involved the young men

you speak of and, others. It was kept private at the time and the 'club' as they called it, was ended and banned from any further activities, upon punishment of being dismissed from the university.

"Three of the young men continued at Cambridge, while Prince Edward departed for his time in the Queen's army."

"What was the tragic episode?" And what might it tell us about what is happening now?

He hesitated, then continued. "Many of our students who did not return home at the week's end of classes frequented a local tavern in Grantchester, very near Cambridge, from time to time. It was well known at the university. The Rose and Crown, as I remember."

"They were young men doing what young men did, as my great aunt had explained it." I commented.

"From time to time, young females from the town would join them." Sir Lowery paused, his gaze met mine.

"There had been rumors of certain activities at the tavern. It seems that one particular night, with an abundance of ale and other spirits, a young local woman was apparently compromised. By more than one young man." He shook his head.

"A dreadful situation that was brought to our attention by the father of the young woman, the vicar of the local church.

"Four young men were identified. They were called in one by one and made to address the claim that was made. It was then that it was learned that several other young men had participated in a sort of contest where bets were made." He shook his head. "Dreadful."

"More than one young man insisted that the young woman made no protest," he continued. "And, in fact, had willingly participated. Still, it would have been a dreadful scandal if the details were made known. Punishments were handed out, a handful departed, including Prince Edward."

The "incident" then covered over as if it never happened.

"Do you remember the name of the young woman?"

"It was not made known by the bishop out of utmost discretion at the time. I do remember hearing that the young woman's father was vicar at St. Andrew and St. Mary's Church at the time. I believe that he left shortly thereafter. No doubt to put the scandal behind them."

"The sins of the fathers will be visited upon the sons."

Was it possible that the vicar, a man of God, but also a father, had decided to take revenge for what happened all those years before? But why now? He would no longer be a young man.

"Will you tell me now, Lady Forsythe, what has brought you here with questions from so long ago?"

Sir Lowery had been forthcoming in answer to my own questions, with information that had been very effectively eliminated from the newspapers, to protect four young men including the Prince of Wales.

We had no proof of anything, yet. Still, I was most grateful for his willingness to share information that might very well have some part in what was happening now.

"There have been three deaths over the past months, two quite recently. In two of those, a note was found that indicated there would be four deaths. Two of the young men were sons of the members of that private club."

He frowned. "I read with great sadness of the death of young Salisbery, a robbery it was said in the daily newspaper. And an accident that claimed the son of Sir Huntingdon several evenings past at Marlborough House."

"From what we have learned, it may very well have been no robbery or accident," I replied.

I didn't go into details, nor did I raise the possibility that there might very well be another accident that was no accident at all and had taken the life of the son of Lord Walsingham.

"Dreadful," he replied.

I thanked Sir Lowery for his time. He stood as we prepared to leave.

"You will let me know more when you can, Lady Forsythe. My wife and I do not have children," he added. "The young men at the university were very much like the sons we never had. I don't suppose you understand."

I assured him that I did and we would let him know. I thanked him then, and Lily and I departed.

"Do ye believe what is happening now is because of what happened all those years before?" Lily asked.

I couldn't be certain. But the conversation with Professor Lowrey most certainly revealed something the Prince of Wales failed to tell us about that incident.

It was late afternoon when we returned to the office on The Strand.

Dark clouds pressed low over the city as we arrived, bringing with them the threat of more rain. Mr. Cavendish was there to inform us that Brodie had returned very near an hour before.

I was most anxious to hear what he might have learned about that woolen scarf Lily found in the forest at Marlborough House. And to share what we had learned.

"You've made it just in time before the storm comes in,"

Mr. Cavendish said as we stepped down from the coach and I paid Mr. Jarvis.

"I've seen it before. There will be snow before mornin'," he added. "Comin' early this season."

I had to agree. It had grown colder the closer we had traveled to the river.

As I turned toward the lift in the alcove, it was there again —a sudden tightness on the back of my neck, almost like a warning.

I searched the street and the sidewalk at the far side, then both directions of The Strand.

Did I see someone there among those who crowded the sidewalk and attempted to wave down a cab before the weather set in?

I saw nothing unusual or that I might have seen before. Still, it was there.

"Are ye all right?" Lily asked.

"Yes, of course. It's just the cold."

Instead of the lift, I took the stairs, which was admittedly far quicker as the first drops of rain fell.

Brodie looked over from the windows on the other side of the office, a frown on his face.

"Weather settin' in."

"It seems we returned just in time," Lily said as she went to the stove to warm her hands.

That dark gaze met mine as he went to the stove and poured a cup of steaming coffee.

In that way that we had become familiar with each other's habits and manner of things, he waited until I had removed my neck scarf and laid it across the coat hook where I'd hung my coat. He handed me the cup, his fingers briefly touching mine.

"Ye're frozen through. Ye should have worn gloves." He pulled his chair to the stove. "Sit and warm yerself."

The coffee was strong, the sort he had once said you might be able to stand a spoon up in. It warmed me through as he poured another cup. He handed it to Lily.

"Ye met with the mother of the young man killed in that riding accident?" he commented as he filled his cup as well.

I nodded and told him about our conversation, and then about the faint marks on the silk shirt her son had worn that day, among things that Lady Walsingham had kept.

Brodie nodded. "Ye believe the marks were made by the same person."

"And perhaps an accident that was no accident at all," I added.

I then told him of our meeting with Sir Lowery, most particularly about that incident that apparently involved all four of the young men involved in betting, members of that notorious club, and apparently with the group forbidden to continue upon threat of dismissal. And shortly thereafter, the Prince of Wales left Trinity.

"The young woman was the daughter of the local cleric at the church in the village. Sir Lowery was not informed of the girl's name, a decision made by the church bishop at the time. However, it might not be difficult to learn the vicar's name," I added.

"Aye," Brodie said with a frown. "It would seem there is a great deal His Highness failed to mention."

Brodie picked up the scarf from Marlborough House and handed it to me.

"I called on Mr. MacInnis at his shop on Bond Street. The cloth was not of a quality he recognized, but most definitely not the sort a gentleman might wear. He suggested that I call on the merchant who supplies wool and other materials to him and other shops, a man by the name of Jesperson.

"He has wool brought from Scotland, the outer islands, and some other finer pieces for special orders. He recognized the material in the scarf. It's not wool, but a specially woven silk."

"Specially woven? For whom?"

"For churches and clerics as part of their vestments," Brodie replied. "Most often with a symbol of the church sewn into it. Yet, there's none on this piece."

Was it possible that the man with the limp Lily had seen escaping from Marlborough House, might be girl's father?

I thought of that first note found on the body of Lord Salisbery's son—not robbery as it was first thought, but murder!

"The sins of the fathers will be visited upon the sons."

Eighteen

LILY STAYED over at the flat next to the office again since
the weather had set in as Mr. Cavendish predicted, turning to
snow as the temperature dropped through the evening.

He had brought us supper from the Public House, then
returned for the night. The hound was presently snoring in
front of the coal stove.

Brodie and I continued to discuss what we had learned
from my visit with Althea Walsingham and the information Sir
Lowery had provided, along with what Brodie had learned
from the wool merchant about the scarf. After supper, I made
notes in my notebook.

"What is to be done now?" Lily asked.

She had listened to our conversation, curious and
thoughtful.

Brodie stood at the window beside his desk, a frown on his
face as he stared out at the snow that came down steadily, occa-
sionally taking a draw from the pipe in his hand.

We had been asked to make inquiries on behalf of the
Prince of Wales after notes were found at the site of two

murders, the second one at Marlborough House the night of the birthday celebration.

However, with what we had now learned, it did seem that His Highness had not been entirely forthcoming in the matter.

But for what purpose? To prevent old secrets being brought to the fore and a possible scandal?

It was one thing to take on an inquiry when provided with everything a prospective client knew or thought they knew. I had experienced that myself in that very first case when my sister disappeared and my great aunt had referred me to a particular private inquiry agent.

It was quite another when information that could be critical to the case had been deliberately withheld, which could be dangerous for all involved. Let alone prevent us from solving the case.

"It does appear that His Highness has chosen to leave out certain information," Brodie said, a fragrant ring of smoke encircling his head as I added notes to my notebook.

"I will contact Sir Knollys in the morning and insist that we meet again."

It was possible that His Highness would be more forthcoming with other information in a conversation with another man. That notion of protecting a woman against possibly shocking and scandalous details.

It was all rubbish of course, as I was not easily offended, particularly after that first case that had taken me into difficult and dangerous situations.

"Do you believe he will tell you the truth of what happened?"

"Perhaps, when I tell him what ye learned today from the vice chancellor of the university."

I had my own thoughts regarding what we had learned. I closed my notebook.

"I believe a trip to Cambridge could be useful," I announced. "The girl's father was the vicar in the local parish. There should be a name in the church records. It could be useful in our search for who is behind these attacks.

"It is not far by rail and worth the trip." I then added something he was not likely to refuse considering recent conversations.

"Lily can go with me. We should be able to return by afternoon. And by then, you may have information from your meeting with His Highness."

Brodie opened then closed his mouth, teeth clamped around the stem of the pipe.

It appeared that I had nipped any argument against it in the bud.

"I've not been to Cambridge yet," Lily said with growing excitement and promptly removed her boots and stockings and set them before the coal stove to dry. "I hope the weather will not prevent it."

"There was no need to include the lass on yer trip to Cambridge," Brodie pointed out as we prepared for bed. "We might have made the trip together the day after, once I've met with His Highness."

If, the Prince of Wales was willing to meet with him.

"I am aware of that," I replied.

It was that hesitation at sending me off on my own that I had experienced before and resigned myself to. Yet, I would not be alone. Lily and I would be traveling and returning the same day.

"I did believe it necessary to rescue you," I commented.

I stepped out of my skirt and laid it over the clothing rack and then unbuttoned my shirt, leaving me in my camisole and underslip.

That dark gaze narrowed on me.

"Rescue? Wot are ye blathering about?"

"From the situation you created by insisting that we include her in our inquiries."

I was right and he knew it.

"As it is, we may learn something in the process." I smiled. "You're quite welcome."

"Ye are a brazen chit," he replied, reaching out and pulling me against him. "I should turn ye over my knee."

As if that would ever happen.

"However..."

"However?"

"Not tonight..."

Lily was already dressed the next morning. She had put more coal on the fire and set the coffee pot to boil. A reminder that she had once performed those duties daily before coming to London.

"A bit late of the mornin' are ye?" she commented as I followed Brodie from the adjoining room.

I caught the look Brodie gave me.

Yes, well, as for turning me over his knee...

"King's Cross station is best for Cambridge," Lily announced. "There are two departures each morning, and the same for the return in the afternoon. Time for travel is little more than an hour."

She then provided both departure times.

"The weather had let up and the messenger office was already open," she announced. "And there are biscuits from the Public House."

"Ye went to the courier office, alone, this time of the mornin'?"

I heard the disapproval in Brodie's voice.

"We will take the second departure," I replied, before that temper could get the better of him.

"That will give us plenty of time to make our inquiries once we arrive, then make the afternoon train back to London."

I handed him a biscuit that contained a thick slice of ham, to soothe the savage beast as it were.

"You might call Sir Knollys at Marlborough House if the telephone is working and make your appointment with His Highness."

Lily grinned.

There were a few comments made, some in Gaelic. From time to time, it was necessary to poke this bear.

"Aye," Brodie said as he set the earpiece back in the cradle on the telephone. "I'm to meet with His Highness at two o'clock this afternoon," he informed me after the call had ended.

"I will see the two of ye to the rail station."

I saw the protest Lily would have made and shook my head.

I did not argue that we were perfectly capable of finding a driver and making the trip to King's Cross station.

"We could take a cab quite easily now that the streets have cleared," she pointed out as we took the lift to the street level while Brodie took the stairs.

"One needs to pick one's battles," I replied.

.   .   .

King's Cross station was very much like a small city under that arched dome with glass panels and included separate tracks for arrivals and departures with an island between.

Under that dome were shops, cafes, a telegraph office, and the ticket office with a half dozen windows.

Coaches with passengers arrived and departed, clogging the roadway that was already congested due to overnight weather and snow.

We had arrived in good time, and Brodie went to purchase our tickets while Lily and I waited under an overhead sign with departure times and destinations.

She had traveled by train to Scotland with us and Aunt Antonia several times, most recently during the influenza outbreak. Yet, there was still that fascination with the congestion of passengers and the sound of trains departing for other places, not to mention the admiration of a young man nearby who made no attempt to disguise his interest in a young girl. Or, rather, a young woman, I reminded myself.

"You seem to have drawn attention," I commented as we waited.

Lily turned to inspect the young man. She might as well have been inspecting fresh produce at a street side vendor, or perhaps the latest catch from a fish monger.

"He's barely out of knickers," she exclaimed. "His mother must be about somewhere."

And so ended that bit of flirtation as Brodie arrived.

"Accordin' to the clerk at the counter, ye should arrive before noon. The last train departs from Cambridge at four o'clock." He handed us our tickets. "The next platform."

He escorted us, then assisted us aboard the train. His hand lingered on mine as Lily continued on into the passenger compartment.

"Be careful."

It was always the same, yet I knew where it came from, and welcomed it. And my response was the same as well.

"Of course."

I watched as he set off, a striking figure, and not at all the sort of "gentleman" other women might prefer. He wore no hat in spite of the weather that morning, taller than those around him, wearing the jumper he preferred to a silk shirt and cravat. And though he was some distance away, there was no disguising the devil's look he gave me now as he turned briefly.

As I turned to enter the passenger compartment I caught a glimpse of a man, simply dressed who quickly slipped through the crowd of passengers on the platform.

His way momentarily blocked, he pushed between a man and woman, ducking his head from sight beneath a cap. He stumbled, then pushed on with some difficulty, and appeared to have a noticeable limp.

I quickly descended the steps onto the platform and searched for sight of him among the crowd of passengers, but he had disappeared.

"Miss?"

I looked up at the rail attendant who now stood on the steps to the rail car.

"The train will be departing. You must board now."

I found the seat Lily had taken with the other across and joined her.

"We should arrive by eleven o'clock," she announced, then looked up.

"Ye look as if ye've seen a ghost, as Mrs. Ryan would say."

Not a ghost, but someone very real I had glimpsed in barely more than a few seconds among a crowd of people?

Surely there was more than one man with limp in all of

London, particularly among those who returned from military service.

We arrived at Cambridgeshire rail station on schedule.

It was a long low, stone building with arches across the front and a carriage barn for passengers who departed, undoubtedly including students who attended Cambridge University as well as local residents. The university, however, was not our destination.

"St. Andrew and St. Mary's Parish church," I told the driver as we climbed aboard a coach. The town of Grantchester was within walking distance of the university with the church beyond.

Lily stared out the window at the sprawling buildings of Cambridge with the dozens of buildings in the Gothic style amid green areas, which included that central tower with the river flowing through.

"That is the university?" Lily asked, obviously quite impressed.

"It's made up of several colleges," I explained. "Over thirty that include the college of medicine, mathematics, and science."

"Did ye attend?" Lily asked.

She was well aware of my time in Paris at private school. However, Cambridge was not part of my education.

How best to respond, I thought, when both my great aunt and I had emphasized the value of an education for her.

"Women are allowed to attend lectures and study," I replied. "However, they are not given certificates for their studies, which would allow them to become doctors."

"But men are given certificates," she concluded. "And become doctors, teachers, and scientists."

I saw the frown that slowly worked its way onto her face.

"How then might a woman support herself? Other than work on the streets?"

That early education of another sort had most definitely not been forgotten.

"They might inherit through their family, or hope to marry," I replied.

"Workhouses, mills, taverns, or places like the one in Edinburgh," she replied.

A "church" of another calling, where we had first met. The frown deepened.

"It's not right."

"No," I agreed. "It is not."

"And yet, ye work with Mr. Brodie, and yer novels have been published quite successfully. That is the reason ye have insisted that I get an education."

"So that you may be able to choose your own path forward and not be forced to rely on someone else," I replied.

It was near midday when we reached the church in Grantchester.

It was made of limestone and fieldstone in a mix of Gothic and earlier Norman styles of the bell tower, arches and tower.

A stone wall surrounded the church cemetery with its ancient headstones. A small red-brick residence with arched windows, perhaps the vicarage, was on the other side of the wall with a gate between.

We left the coach at the end of the cobbled walkway that the led across the church yard to a small stone entryway that led into the church proper.

"I've not been in a *real* church before," Lily whispered.

She was, of course, referring to the "Church" in Edinburgh, an abandoned church that had been turned into a whorehouse where she had worked as a lady's maid.

"Good afternoon," we were greeted. "I am Reverend Jeffers. Welcome to St. Andrew and St. Mary's."

I introduced us to him. "I hope we are not interrupting."

There had been no service or meeting noted on the board at the entryway.

"We had early morning service for those who attend. The next service is this evening."

"We've traveled from London," I explained. "I'm hoping you can assist us with information from some time ago."

He was quite young, although with that sort of calm demeanor I had found in other members of clergy, along with a friendly smile, and a warm brown gaze.

"I have only been here for two years; therefore, I am not certain how much assistance I might be." He then asked us to follow him to his office in the rectory.

"You say this is from some time ago," he said as he sat behind the plain desk. A crucifix hung on the wall, several leather-bound books on a reading table that included what appeared to be a Bible that lay open.

"I read daily," he explained. "To remind myself of my own faults. It helps me understand the troubles that people bring to the church." He smiled. "Now, I will try to help if I can."

"We are making inquiries on behalf of someone who attended university quite some time ago," I explained. "It would be helpful if we knew who the vicar was here at that time."

He nodded. "There is a record in the bishop's office, of course. That might provide the information you're looking for. There is a record of documents that are kept here at the

Church—for births, marriages, deaths in the parish, that would include those who presided over them. It might be possible to learn the vicar's name from those records." He rose from behind his desk and went to that table.

"What is the year?"

I replied that it would be 1860 or 1861.

He opened one of those leather-bound ledger.

"There are records from as early as the eleventh century, barely legible I must confess. I have found them most interesting. This particular one contains more recent entries for the past hundred years for residents of the parish."

"Excuse me for interrupting." A young woman appeared in the doorway of the rectory. "I didn't know you had visitors."

"Not at all, Livvy." Reverend Jeffers introduced us. "My wife, Mrs. Jeffers. I was just assisting these ladies with a bit of church history," he explained.

His wife smiled. "It is Mrs. Kearney. She is having some difficulty and has asked to speak with you. She is quite upset."

"Ah, confessor for students, wayward souls, and marriage counselor. By all means, where might I find Mrs. Kearney?"

"She is in the small chapel," his wife replied.

He excused himself then. "You are welcome to search the records" he told us in parting.

"I thought vicars could not marry," Lily commented after he left.

"They are allowed to in the Anglican church. Catholic priests are not allowed to marry."

"If priests are not allowed, how are they supposed to help someone like that woman, Mrs. Kearney?"

A very good question, I thought as I stepped to the table with the ledger and adjusted the light over for a better view.

I understood her confusion. Religion could be difficult to

understand, particularly when one had been influenced by a woman who planned a Viking sendoff as I had been. And now Lily as well.

The entries I scanned in the recorded information were for the year 1860 and in Latin. Not unexpected.

I was hoping to find entries for April and May of 1861, which would have been at the time of that incident.

"I found a name however. All these entries are for 1860. The vicar at the time was J. Hollings."

Lily opened the next ledger and began scanning the entries. I saw the confusion at her face.

"It's written in Latin," I explained.

She wrinkled her nose in frustration.

"Aprilis and Maius," I translated. "Very similar to English, look for the year 1861 as well."

She continued reading through the entries. The wrinkle eventually disappeared.

"I found the entries for April that year," she announced excitedly. "The vicar's name was Chastain? The name is on the entire page and then after."

I peered over her shoulder. There were entries with that name well into the months of September and October. Then another name had been entered.

"Not even a year later? What does that mean?"

Reverend Jeffers had told us that those assigned to the church served three years and then moved on to another parish. Reading through these entries, it did seem that Reverend Chastain had either turned over his position or left St. Andrew and St. Mary's at the end of October of 1861.

"I do apologize," Reverend Jeffers said as he returned. "Mrs. Kearney was in quite a state, a frequent occurrence I'm afraid."

"We found what we were looking for," I replied. "Reverend Chastain apparently left October 1861. Would there be a record where he was assigned next?"

"That would be in the records kept by the bishop as well. However, there is someone in the village who might know more about that. Mrs. Hollings has been here for decades, one of our oldest members—ninety-six years old. She fancies herself as sort of a church historian, if you will. She lives just up the High Road toward the village, a cottage with a slate roof.

"I could send a note of introduction if you want to call on her. It's not far."

"Ninety-six years old," Lily exclaimed after Mrs. Jeffers told us a little bit more about the church's "historian." "I didn't know anyone lived that long."

I didn't either, however, it did seem as if my great aunt at the age of eighty-seven was going to give it a go.

With that note of introduction in hand, we left St. Andrew and St. Mary's church and walked toward the village where we easily found Mrs. Hollings cottage.

It was small but tidy with a fence around the yard and faced the street. A middle-aged woman, her housekeeper perhaps, met us at the door. At ninety-six, I thought Mrs. Hollings was entitled to a little help.

"Who is at the door, Annie?"

"Visitors from the church. They have a note from Reverend Jeffers."

The cottage was small, the kitchen adjoining the room with a hearth and two overstuffed chairs, a small bedroom just beyond.

A tiny woman sat in one of the chairs with a blanket across her lap, a scraggly grey dog at her feet. Her housekeeper handed her the note Reverend Jeffers had written.

She read it, then looked at us. "My eyes are not what they used to be," she said with a frown.

"What do ye call him?" Lily asked as she bent to pet the dog.

"What is that, you say?" Mrs. Hollings replied.

"He must have a name."

The dog caught her scent and immediately began to wag his tail.

"He has a name—Otis. He doesn't usually take to strangers. And you would be Mikaela Forsythe and Miss Lily Montgomery," Mrs. Hollings commented with note in hand and apparently no difficulty reading our names after all.

"Sit," she said then. "Annie will bring tea and then you can tell me what you want to know about St. Andrew and St. Mary's."

As before, I explained that we were looking for information about the man who was vicar in the early months of 1861, and the name we found in the church records

She nodded. "That would be the Reverend Chastain, and a dreadful time for the parish with the scandal that involved those boys from the university."

Historian indeed, I thought. "What can you tell us about that?"

"It involved several well-placed young men, very nearly got themselves dismissed," she added with a nod. "There were four of them, called themselves..."

"The Four Horsemen," I provided.

"That was it! Some sort of biblical reference, caused quite a stir at the time. But not nearly as much as the scandal over that poor girl, the vicar's daughter, no less. Mary was her name.

"Not that I was surprised," she said with a knowing look. "She was a wild young thing, the mother passed on. But the worst of it was that night at the Rose and Crown, the tavern at the other end of the village near the university.

"Those young men closed the tavern down, some twenty odd of them, including the young prince. It was said the girl was there as well. As I said, wild, if you get my meanin'.

"There was all sorts of gossip that went on that night, and His Highness was removed from the university shortly afterward by his father. It was said that he was sent out of the country to protect him against any scandal.

"It was a short while after that Mr. Chastain put in a request to end his term so that he could leave with the girl. The bishop agreed, and they were gone shortly after. I felt sorry for them both. Mr. Jewett came in after, a good man, bless his soul."

"Do you know where Mr. Chastain and his daughter might have gone?"

"St. Pancras Old Church at Camden, according to Emma Mayhew. Her sister was housekeeper at the rectory there for some time, though I'm certain she has passed on now. She was older than me." She cackled with laughter. "If you can imagine."

We now had more information than when we arrived—a name and where the vicar had gone at the time. No doubt to avoid a scandal that the bishop at the time hoped to avoid.

"What sort of person was the vicar?" I asked. She had spoken a great deal about Mary, but little about her father.

"A good man as well, he doted on the girl. Did his best, I suppose, to raise her without the mother about. Not an easy task, as I well know."

"Was there any mention about either of them after they left?"

"It all quieted down afterward. Mr. Jewett, who came in

after, was a single man and did not tolerate gossip that involved the church."

We stood to leave.

"I appreciate the visit. You will be taking the train back to London then?" she commented.

"It's a short walk from here to the village," she added. "I go two, sometimes three, times a week to market. Though the weather is fixing to set in."

I thanked her for the tea as Lily said good-bye to Otis.

"She walks there two or three times a week?" Lily commented as we left. "She reminds me of Lady Montgomery."

We reached the rail station in good time and purchased luncheon at a restaurant as we warmed ourselves and waited for the afternoon train.

On the return to London, Lily made notes on the information we'd learned.

We had learned a great deal, yet as with past inquiry cases, it raised an entirely new set of questions.

Was the Reverend Chastain still in London? Had he retired from the church and perhaps moved elsewhere? What had happened to Mary Chastain?

We arrived late afternoon back in London and found a driver to make the trip to the office on The Strand.

Mr. Cavendish informed us that Brodie had left earlier for the meeting with the Prince of Wales at Marlborough House. He then handed an envelope to me.

"This arrived this morning by courier."

The envelope was the usual envelope used by the courier services around the city. Inside was another envelope, of the sort used as personal stationery. A note was written across the front of the envelope.

"I found this in my husband's desk." And the initials, *A.W.*

I opened the inside envelope. It was from Lady Walsingham.

A note was enclosed. It was smudged with dirt but still legible.

"The sins of the fathers shall be visited upon the sons"

And below that, another cryptic message:

"And then there were three"

With that cryptic message resembling the other notes that had been left on the bodies of two young men, it had obviously been found on Lady Walsingham's son the day of the accident.

From the note she had written on the outside of the envelope, it appeared that she had searched for it after we met. And it seemed that the son of Sir Walsingham, one of those four young men years before, had been the first victim, followed then by the deaths of two more—the son of Lord Salisbery, and the death only days earlier of the son of Sir Huntingdon.

Three.

I thought of what had started our search, something my great aunt mentioned in passing that had disappeared from any mention in the dailies at the time, or any time afterward.

They had called themselves the Four Horsemen, those four sons of privilege, and the sort of foolish things those young men did. Foolishness, we had learned, that had led to the compromise of a young woman and the threat of scandal. That young woman, Mary Chastain, had left Grantchester and the scandal along with her father.

Now, after more than thirty years, the sons of three of

those foolish young men were dead. With perhaps a fourth son to meet the same fate?

A father's vengeance after all this time?

"What is to be done now?" Lily asked as I sat at the desk while we waited for Brodie to return from his meeting with Prince Edward.

Nineteen

MARLBOROUGH HOUSE

BRODIE LOOKED up as the motion of the coach changed, and the driver slowed the team at the gate.

He provided his name and informed the uniformed guard that he had an appointment with His Highness. It seemed that a message had been provided to the guards, a list checked, and then the driver was waved through.

He had gone back through the information the Prince of Wales had provided since taking the inquiry case, along with information they had learned that had not yet been made known.

Brodie understood the need for discretion. He had encountered that before in his time as an inspector with the MET and after taking on certain cases when he left the Metropolitan.

Most particularly with a first case for Lady Antonia and then a second one to retrieve her niece who had gone astray on some island.

There had been the need for discretion as well, in a previous inquiry case regarding a threat against the royal family.

And now, as Mikaela often said? An accident the night of the birthday celebration that was no accident, a note left on the young man's body with that unusual message, and an attack days earlier on another young man outside his club during a robbery with another note:

"Sins of the fathers."

A biblical reference according to Mikaela. And then Lady Antonia had spoken of an incident more than thirty years before. Brash university students, full of themselves, as Mikaela described, and their club with exclusive membership:

"The Four Horsemen."

His own knowledge of the Bible sorely lacking, Mikaela had explained the meaning of it, from the book of Revelations, The Four Horsemen of the Apocalypse.

The Prince of Wales hadn't mentioned it, nor anything of that particular incident when he had suddenly departed university for the military, followed by an extended time away—traveling across Europe.

Brodie stepped down from the coach and was greeted by another set of uniformed guards at the entrance of Marlborough House. He presented his calling card to another guard.

"I will inform Sir Knollys."

The official gatekeeper. What did the personal secretary to the Prince of Wales know about that time and the incident they'd discovered with their inquiries? An incident that, it was undoubtedly hoped, would never be made known?

There were always secrets, he had his own. Everyone had things they preferred to be left unknown.

What would the Prince of Wales be willing to tell him now?

Sir Knollys had appeared and greeted him with that same closed expression and polite words.

"His Royal Highness will see you now."

He was escorted to the library where they had previously met. Sir Knollys announced his arrival, then discreetly left, closing the door behind him.

The Prince of Wales sat at his desk; papers spread in front of him as before. He wore a formal suit of clothes, as he had when they last met, a medallion of some sort over the breast pocket of his jacket. His beard was neatly trimmed as he frowned over those papers.

It was several moments before His Highness looked up and acknowledged him.

"Mr. Brodie..." he glanced past him and commented. "Lady Forsythe has not accompanied you."

"No, sir. An appointment in the matter of our inquiries needed her attention elsewhere," he explained, matter of fact.

"Is there some progress in the situation?" Prince Edward inquired.

"There is."

When he said nothing further, His Highness finally looked up. He laid his pen at the desk, then sat back in his desk chair.

"By all means continue," he said. "And we can hopefully be done with this dreadful business."

"Wot can you tell me, sir, about the particular incident that led to you leaving university?"

Silence filled the library except for the sound of the clock on the wall as the prince's gaze met his.

In that moment, they were simply two men, no more, one tasked with finding the truth, the other with secrets.

"You have been most diligent, Mr. Brodie." His Highness pushed away from the desk and stood.

He paced across the library until he stood before the windows, staring out at the massive green and the forest beyond where Lily had chased after the man she'd seen at the gallery the night of the birthday celebration.

"A long time ago," Edward finally replied. "The foolishness of young men. You perhaps understand, Mr. Brodie."

"The sins of the fathers...?" he repeated what was written in that first note.

His Highness flinched. "What have you learned?"

"What you might have shared from the beginning, sir."

Brodie saw the control His Highness asserted in the way he straightened his shoulders, his frown. And perhaps denial of any knowledge of it?

He was prepared to walk out of the library and be done with it all. Let Sir Avery continue with his inquiries. Brodie would not be persuaded otherwise, to simply overlook certain matters.

"What happened at university all those years before?" he inquired. "I must know all of it before we can continue."

His Highness returned to his desk and slowly sat in that chair. He leaned back, eyes closed for those few moments.

There was no pretense: no posturing as Brodie might have expected.

Sir Knollys returned as if at some previously agreed time.

"All is well," His Highness assured his personal secretary. "We will have coffee, and please cancel my meetings for the rest of the afternoon."

〜

#204 THE STRAND

After arriving back in London, Lily and I returned to the office.

We spent the remainder of the afternoon going over every-thing we'd learned from our trip to Grantchester in our search for information about that night over thirty years earlier.

According to what Mrs. Hollings had shared, the vicar at the time, Reverend Chastain, had been assigned to St. Pancras Old Church in London by special order of the archbishop after that dreadful situation with his daughter.

The church where he had then taken up service was in an older part of London, some distance from The Strand.

According to what Lily and I had learned, those who served the church did so for a term of three years, usually assigned elsewhere afterward.

How long had Mr. Chastain been at St. Pancras? Had he continued on, or left at the end of his term? If so, where might he have gone?

It was possible that his daughter might have eventually married after leaving Cambridge.

Would there be a record of it? If she had not married, then what had happened to her?

I knew from past inquiry cases that girls who had suffered such things often ended up on the streets.

What was Mary Chastain's fate?

And now, all these years later, who was responsible for the murders of three young men whose fathers were connected to that horrible episode?

What was the motive? I thought not for the first time: A father's revenge? But why after all these years?

Blackmail made sense, yet no blackmail demand had been made to our knowledge.

I put down my pen and closed my notebook. Perhaps Brodie might learn something in his meeting with His Highness.

It had been hours since we had eaten last in that rail station cafe in Cambridge. Food was most definitely in order. We left word with Mr. Cavendish and set off across The Strand to the Public House.

The food there was simple but hearty, more the sort favored by workers at end of day. We both ordered meat pie.

"Not to forget, miss," Miss Effie reminded us. "We have the chapel at All Saints for the eighth of December."

Miss Effie and Mr. Cavendish were to be married on that date.

What began as simple friendship had grown deeper for both of them, although the proposal had come from Miss Effie as Mr. Cavendish was convinced no one would ever want to be with a man who had lost both legs.

Miss Effie, a woman of strong character, had been forced to take the matter into her hands, so to speak—she had proposed to *him*, insisting that he make an honest woman of her.

I was pleased for them. It was clear to anyone who knew them that they were quite taken with each other. Brodie had been hesitant.

"How the devil will he provide for them?" he said at the time when the announcement was made. "With the small amount she's no doubt paid at the Public House?"

I did see his point.

"There is a simple solution," I told him. "You must increase what we pay Mr. Cavendish for his services here. With what she makes, they should be able to manage quite well."

I pointed out that it was not unlike our own arrangement with the trust that had been set up for my sister and I, along with substantial royalties from my books. In addition, I might provide Mr. Cavendish with additional funds as his responsibilities to us have increased substantially, that included his resources on the street for information.

"I can well afford to compensate him, and take care of ye as well," Brodie replied. "I've no need of yer money."

An argument in the past.

"You must tell him straightaway," I told him. "Or I can deliver the news if you prefer. It will make them both very happy."

He glared at me at the time, that dark look that was hardly intimidating.

"How did I lose the argument?" he demanded then.

So, here we were with the month of December, the holidays, and a wedding rapidly approaching.

Lily and I had only just returned to the office on The Strand, when the service bell rang on the landing. Brodie arrived, a frown at his mouth.

It did appear it had been a difficult meeting with His Highness, one that had gone on quite long.

I had stoked the fire in the coal stove when Lily and I returned from the Public House. Brodie removed his long coat, then went to the stove and extended his hands toward heat.

"We brought supper for ye," Lily commented.

He eventually looked up. "Aye."

I sensed it was not food he needed at present and went to the cabinet that sat against the wall adjacent to his desk. I retrieved a bottle of Old Lodge whisky and poured a dram into a tumbler. I handed it to him.

A faint smile made it past the frown as he took the tumbler, then tossed back the contents.

"A difficult meeting?" I inquired.

He held out the tumbler for another dram.

"Aye."

He had said before leaving that we would not continue if His Highness was not forthcoming with answers to the questions he intended to ask.

I had prepared myself for it, although I did not agree, considering what Lily and I had learned on our trip to Cambridge.

"It seems there was considerably more His Highness chose not to tell us about the matter." He stared down into the glass as he swirled the contents about. "I informed him that we would make no further inquiries unless he told me everything."

I could only imagine how that might have been received, no doubt a surprise for someone who was used to being obeyed in all things.

I did admire Brodie for his forthright manner. He would have called it *being direct,* something he had pointed out about myself more than once.

I waited as the whisky had its way, smoothing the edges so to speak.

"It seems that he was contacted several months ago by the person who may be responsible for the murders," he began, having drained his glass once more.

"A matter usually handed off to those in his staff who are familiar with such things. It was not until the incident outside White's and that particular note was discovered that it seemed the threat might be verra real."

"And he then contacted us to investigate the so-called 'robbery,'" I concluded the obvious.

"At the time, he claims that he thought it much the same as with her ladyship, someone who had learned about the rumors of that incident years before and determined to make profit from it."

"Except there was no demand for payment," I suggested from what we knew. "And then the incident at Marlborough House happened."

He nodded. "And another note that was obviously part of it."

I went to my desk and retrieved the note I had received from Lady Walsingham. I handed it to him.

"It seems that she found it in Sir Walsingham's desk after I met with her."

"Aye, another piece of the puzzle, as ye like to call it.

"And then there were three."

Yet, apparently not sent for blackmail in that instance either.

I explained our visit with the vicar at the church in Grantchester and our search of the parish records there.

"Chastain?"

"He was vicar there for less than a year, then suddenly left after the incident."

"There is a woman in the village who remembered," Lily added. "The archbishop arranged for the vicar to leave and take a new assignment."

"He was sent here," I added. "To St. Pancras."

Brodie frowned. "He would be quite old now."

I had thought that as well. If he was still with the church there.

"What of the daughter?" he inquired. "Was there any word about her?"

"She went with him. As you can well imagine, she would have had few prospects after what happened. Although she might have married after arriving here.

"We also learned that each vicar is given a three-year term, then sent on to another parish," I went on to explain. "There should be a record of where he was sent after he left there, if he did at all."

I had already decided that Lily and I would go to St. Pancras in the morning, as it was still the middle of the week, and there would be no scheduled church services to interrupt.

Brodie nodded. "It could be useful to speak with someone there."

At the same time, I sensed there was something else from his visit with the Prince of Wales.

"I learned something more in my conversation with His Highness," he said. "It seems there was a man who was in service at Marlborough House until a few weeks ago and then left. A stableman according to Sir Knollys."

Another detail that His Highness had not mentioned or did not know about at the time, in that way that things regarding servants and staff were handed off to others.

"Was there a description of the man?"

"He was described as tall, thick set, and verra strong, according to the stablemaster. He was quiet spoken in his manner, and he knew his way around horses."

Someone who might have assisted the murderer in his escape that night at Marlborough House?

Had I seen a man who fit that description?

Admittedly, the street and sidewalk had been crowded at the end of the day and the weather dreadful. It was only a glimpse, and then he had disappeared.

"I may have seen the man Lily described."

That dark gaze narrowed.

"Where?"

I explained about the man who resembled that description, whom I had seen across the way from the office. I went on to describe the other suspect from my brief encounter at the rail station before Lily and I departed for Cambridge. A man who appeared to have a limp, and had then disappeared.

Twenty

LILY HAD STAYED OVER AGAIN. And the office
was somewhat nearer for our trip to St. Pancras Old Church to
see what might be learned about the vicar, Mr. Chastain.

I made a telephone call to the parish church first thing in
the morning and spoke with a clerk. As it was early and the
middle of the week, there were no church services scheduled
for the day.

She was to go me. We were given a time of one o'clock to
meet with the vicar. Brodie was also to accompany us. He
insisted after I had spoken of the two encounters—one across
from the office and the other at King's Cross station, before we
left for Cambridge.

We ate at the Public House, then returned to the office on
The Strand. Mr. Cavendish had just returned from the lift and
met us at the entrance to the office.

"I took a message up to the landing. Appears to be from
that man at the Agency. The bloody machine stopped twice
between the ground floor and the second."

The bloody machine being the lift. There have been some difficulties with it since it was installed.

As for the message that had been received, it appeared that it was from Sir Avery Stanton.

"Best take the stairs, miss," he cautioned. "Or you might find yourselves trapped in the thing. I'll send word round for people to repair it."

Brodie followed on the stairs, his preferred means of traversing from street to the office. There was a frown on his face as he retrieved the envelope Mr. Cavendish had left.

Lily and I entered ahead. I set my umbrella in the stand, then removed my long coat and hung it on the coat rack.

Brodie's frown deepened as he read the note, followed by a curse. He was not pleased.

"An official summons from His Highness for a meeting with the Home Secretary, and Sir Avery is to be included." He thrust the note at me.

It was for this morning, and not something that could be declined, unless one found oneself run over by an omnibus or bound and thrown into the river.

Brodie looked over at me.

"Ye should wait until I return to go to St. Pancras, then I can go with ye."

"It is the middle of the day. There will be others about. I doubt we will be in any danger in a church," I replied. "And I do have the revolver."

I was most anxious to learn what we might find there, particularly with the risk to the son of the fourth member of that exclusive club, the Duke of York.

"It would be far simpler, Mikaela Forsythe, if ye were a docile creature who did the laundry and cooking, and then waited for her husband to come home each day."

Lily smothered a laugh.

"First of all, Mr. Brodie, the few times I have attempted laundry—one of them in a somewhat urgent situation that involved your shirt—you will admit that it was a disaster," I replied. "The shirt had ended in the rag bin, a glorious shade of pink."

"Aye."

"Second, my attempts at cooking have not fared better. I have more pressing things to do than measuring this or that, then hovering over a hot stove all day."

Although not for lack of trying, with a roast chicken that was somewhat the worst for it afterward and provided Rupert with a tasty meal. But then, he'd been known to eat any foul thing found on the street.

"I am aware of yer lack of abilities in that area," he commented. "It is a wonder either of us have survived yer attempts."

"And third," I had saved this for last. "I have never been considered docile, nor am I one to simply wait at home for the master of the house to return. In conclusion, Mr. Brodie, you knew very well I did not possess, nor was likely to ever possess, any of those qualities when you proposed to me."

"It must have been momentary insanity." He pulled me against him.

I fought to control the laugher. "Momentary insanity?"

"Or a wee bit longer. I'm not certain there's a cure." He kissed me quite thoroughly.

Lily smothered a laugh behind her hand.

Brodie finally set me from him.

"And I presume there's no talking ye out of going to St. Pancras," he presumed correctly.

"Not at all," I finally managed to say. "We will be there and back in short order. Perhaps even before your return from meeting with the Home Secretary."

He read the note again.

"You might want to dress more formally for your meeting with the Home Secretary," I suggested.

We had both met Henry Matthews, the present Home Secretary, in a previous inquiry.

He was quite formal in his manner, yet not the sort to look down on those who were not of the peerage, and had highly valued our participation in a particular case at the time. He had left the position of Home Secretary the year before, then was called back to his present term by Mr. Gladstone.

"Aye," Brodie replied as he retreated to the adjacent room.

When he eventually emerged, he had been transformed into the very striking image of a gentleman, albeit with tie in hand.

"I can never tie the bloody thing," he grumbled, and would have tossed it aside.

I retrieved it. I felt that dark gaze on me as I very efficiently tied it for him. When I had completed the task and would have stepped back, his hand covered mine and he stopped me.

"Be careful."

"Of course. After all, who else would tie your tie when you are summoned to the Home Office?" I replied.

"Perhaps a woman on the street corner," he suggested.

"Who would tolerate that Scots temper?"

The answer was in the half smile at one corner of his mouth. "Aye."

"You would do well to remember that, sir."

He held onto my hand a moment longer.

"Whatever ye learn, ye're to return here and not set off on yer own."

"Of course, dear."

"We should leave no later than eleven o'clock because of the weather," I told Lily after he had gone.

"It's only a few miles, but that will give us plenty of time with traffic and depending on the road condition."

She grinned at me. "Of course."

St. Pancras Old Church was not far as the crow flies, according to that old saying. Less than three miles.

However, the way was often crowded with traffic, routes that changed due to the extension of the rail line, and then there was the weather.

Mr. Cavendish was able to secure the service of Mr. Jarvis once more. He was knowledgeable of most areas of London, and I was confident he would see us safely there.

Lily and I climbed aboard. Rupert the hound immediately followed and grinned up at us as he sat on the floor of the coach between us.

"Mr. Brodie might have mentioned that the hound should accompany you," Mr. Cavendish commented as he closed the door of the coach.

And pigs fly, I thought.

"It must be comforting to have someone who cares so about you," Lily commented as we set off.

I smiled to myself. It was.

We encountered no delays and arrived well in time for our meeting with the vicar. I asked Mr. Jarvis to wait.

True to his nature, the hound was excited to explore the churchyard that surrounded St. Pancras Church.

We were met by the clerk of the church as we stepped inside and were informed that the vicar had been called to a meeting at Westminster. However, the clerk, a slender young man by the name of James with a kind smile, had been authorized to assist us in whatever we needed.

"If you will follow me, the church records are in the library."

The original church of St. Pancras was several hundred years old, with the new section added early in the 19th century that included a sanctuary, chancel, and nave.

We passed the sanctuary where a sign noted that service would be held on the following Friday and then on Sunday as usual. Otherwise, it was quite empty.

The library was in what remained of the Old Church with hand-carved stone walls, the faint echo of our footsteps on the stone floor, and the familiar smell of books, hundreds of them.

"I'm told that it was far easier to keep this as the library, rather than rebuild it and then move all the books. Some of these are hundreds of years old from when the old church was founded," the clerk explained.

"The records you are looking for should be here as all records of the church have been meticulously preserved."

Following our trip to Cambridge, and St. Andrew and St. Mary's church in Grantchester, Lily and I were quite familiar with church records.

"I took the liberty of pulling the records that cover the years the new church was built until present. They're on this table. The vicar, Mr. Powell, indicated these should provide the information you're looking for."

"I will leave you to your search, as I have work in the office," he explained. "I will return later if you have any questions."

The records had been laid out on a reading table with an electric lamp. We both removed our coats before sitting at the table. I took my notebook from my bag and smiled as Lily did the same. We each spread a large leather-bound book filled with entries.

The beginning date of the one before me was 1762. The entries included a record of births, marriages, deaths, and the dates a new vicar arrived with an occasional entry noting the departure date of a prior vicar, Henry Winston.

He had arrived in May 1784, for a period of almost ten years! He departed for a new parish in June 1793, with the new vicar arriving a month prior, according to what had been written there.

There were other entries for clerks and the occasion of a visit by the bishop of the archdiocese as well as visits by notable persons, including a visit by the Duke of Kent, Queen Victoria's father, April 1816. Most were written in Latin.

I quickly scanned each page as the years passed, the archive ending in January of 1860.

"It must be in the one you have," I told Lily as I closed the book I'd searched. "An entry could have been made any time in 1861 or perhaps 1862, depending on the church record-keeping."

It was tedious, although I was grateful for my ability to translate Latin, while Lily was unusually quiet.

"I can't read most of this," she finally said. "The year for each one is written in Latin as well."

I glanced over her shoulder.

"Look for the Reverend Chastain's name," I suggested. "That should be easier."

"I found it," she eventually announced.

I translated the remainder of the entry. "The Reverend Joseph Chastain, Vicar, arrived 8 September 1861."

"Continue searching for when he might have been sent to a

new parish," I told her as I opened my notebook and entered the date she'd found.

"The usual term is three years before being assigned elsewhere. That might be sometime in 1864, or possibly later."

She continued to scan the entries on the following pages.

"I didn't find anything," she eventually announced.

Was it possible Reverend Chastain had remained longer?

"He might have stayed on," I suggested. "It's possible there was no one to assume the position at that time." I stood with her then, reading through the entries as well.

"There." I pointed to an entry dated 16 May 1866.

It appeared that Reverend Chastain had remained at St. Pancras an additional two years past his normal term.

As with the other entries made by hand, the ink had faded as the paper in the archives aged. It was difficult to read the note that had been added. Lily moved the lamp closer.

"What else does it say?" Lily asked.

"*Faithful servant in the Lord's service,*" I translated. "*Departed this date for St. Mary's Church, Hendon.*"

Lily had done well. At least now we knew when Reverend Chastain had left, but what of his daughter who had suffered so horribly?

"Did you find any reference for Mary Chastain?"

Lily shook her head. "The vicar's name was the only one."

A sound beyond the library caught both of our attention. I glanced at the clock on the wall of the library.

It had grown quite late. The clerk had been gone for quite some time and should have returned.

"We have what we came for, we should leave. If we see the clerk on our way, we will thank him." I pulled on my coat and tucked my notebook into my bag as Lily did the same.

"It's quite late," she whispered as we retraced out steps in the darkened hallway. "And there's no one about."

There was another sound now, very nearby. I thought of Brodie's warning.

Was someone there, just behind us, moving swiftly now in our direction? I quickened our steps, and Lily as well.

We reached the end of the hallway and a hand reached out.

"Lady Forsythe."

It was James, the clerk of the church.

"I was just on my way to see if you needed any assistance. It's quite late and I will be leaving soon."

"I thought that you might have returned earlier," I suggested with a glance back down the hallway. "There was someone very near the library."

He shook his head. "I have only just returned after assisting one of our parishioners."

"I must be mistaken," I said.

Except that I was certain I was not. There had definitely been someone in the hallway.

"At this time of the day and the middle of the week, I'm the only one here," he explained. "Except for the groundskeeper."

Lily started to protest. She had heard that sound as well.

While I would have liked very much to know who was there, I wasn't willing to risk any harm to Lily. And it did seem that whoever had been there was not there now. I only hoped that Mr. Jarvis was still waiting with the coach.

I thanked James once more and we quickly left.

"There was someone there," Lily said quite vehemently. "We should find them."

"We need to leave!" I replied.

"But what if it was the man you saw before?"

Precisely, I thought.

Mr. Jarvis was there, the coach silhouetted against a dark grey sky as snow began to fall once more. And somewhere on the church grounds I heard the sound of a hound baying quite furiously.

Lily gave a sharp whistle, then another.

Rupert eventually appeared, though reluctantly as he stopped more than once at full attention in the direction he had come.

Lily whistled once more, and he returned to the coach.

We quickly climbed inside, and I asked Jarvis to take us to Sussex Square.

"Sussex Square?" Lily said. "We should return to the office so that we can let Brodie know what we learned."

"It would be best if you return to Sussex Square," I replied. Where she would be safe. Munro would be there.

She was not pleased.

"Why are ye sending me back?" she demanded. "Haven't I shown ye that I can be helpful. I found the information about Reverend Chastain being sent to St. Mary's in Hendon."

The Scots accent slipped through again as I had noticed before when she was in a temper.

"Mr. Brodie said..."

"He would not want you to pursue this now," I interjected. "We don't yet know what this is all about."

I thought of those cryptic notes that had been left on the bodies and the additional ones sent to His Highness.

"Three young men have been murdered."

"There may very well will be another attempt."

"I don't need yer protection," she argued as we continued toward Sussex Square. "I'm not a child. I can take care of myself. Ye are not my mother!"

She stopped herself and stared at me across the darkened interior of the coach, her expression quite different now.

"I didn't mean that...I apologize."

"I have never thought of you as a child," I replied. "But that does not mean that I do not care what happens to you."

I was very aware that I could not prevent her choosing her own path. "I ask that you trust me in this."

She eventually nodded, however she was silent for the rest of the trip to Sussex Square and then once again after we arrived.

Brodie came out of the office as Mr. Jarvis delivered the hound and I safely back to The Strand.

He took one look at me and frowned as he came down the stairs, then paid Mr. Jarvis.

"Aye, dinna stand there in the cold." He took my hand.

Twenty-One

BRODIE CALLED it my woman's intuition.

It appeared that I was far more correct than I would have liked in my conversation with Lily.

An attempt had been made upon the Duke of York, the son of His Highness, and his young wife as they returned the previous evening to their apartments at St. James's Palace.

The attack had come on the street as they returned from a reception at Buckingham Palace, an incredibly bold attempt, not unlike the attack on the son of Lord Salisbery as he had departed White's Club.

It explained the urgent meeting that Brodie was called to earlier.

"Was anyone harmed?"

"The guards around the Duke of York had been increased. One of them got in a blow before the man managed to escape with the aid of another."

"Was either man seen?"

"There was not enough light with the weather and the late

hour of the night. But the man who attacked the duke had an obvious impairment of one leg."

"What of the man who helped him escape?" I then asked.

I was certain I already knew the answer—a tall man and thick set.

I explained the feeling there was someone outside of the church's library. And my decision for Lily to return to Sussex Square. And Rupert was quite insistent in the graveyard as if there was someone there.

"Aye, it was right ye did so. She is headstrong, that one."

I then told him what we had learned from the church records.

"St. Mary's Church?" he remarked. "That could tell us more, but not tonight," he added as he pushed aside the heavy drapes at the office window.

"No one will be out and about, wot with the weather."

The lights in the office flickered and then went out leaving us in darkness except for the fire in the coal stove.

He attempted to place a telephone call to Sir Avery to tell him what I had learned. But it appeared that, along with the electric, the service for the telephone had also become a victim of the weather that had steadily worsened after I left Sussex Square.

Rain beat against the office window and filled the street below, a risky enterprise for anyone who ventured out as traffic thinned.

It did appear that a good part of the rest of The Strand was without electric as well, except for gas streetlights in the theatre district in the distance.

Then the sound of the rain eased and turned to snow.

I retrieved an oil lamp from the cabinet, left from some-what more primitive conditions only the year before, and lit it as Brodie set the lock on the door. He then added more coal to the fire in the stove.

"The mornin' will be here soon enough," he said, as he poked at the fire. I sat at my desk and opened my notebook and made notes in the pool of light from the stove.

It was sometime later that he added more coal to the fire, then went to the cupboard adjacent to his desk.

"Stale biscuits and whisky," he announced.

I set my pen down. It wasn't the first time we had only biscuits and some of my great aunt's whisky.

"Yes, please," I replied.

He poured us both a dram, handed a tumbler to me, then set the carton of stale biscuits on my desk.

I munched—it was good that I had strong teeth—then took a sip of Old Lodge whisky.

"Is it possible that Reverend Chastain is behind the murders?" I asked him. "Revenge for what happened to his daughter, even though that was over thirty years ago?"

A strong motive, as we had seen in previous inquiry cases.

"Perhaps," Brodie replied as he bit off a piece of biscuit.

"I suppose it is possible that the man who's been doing this might be the husband of Mary Chastain," I said as I thought of what we knew.

"Aye, perhaps."

"She could be living somewhere here in London and her husband learned of it..."

"Perhaps."

That was the third *"perhaps,"* an obvious sign that he was deep in his own thoughts.

He tossed back the last of the whisky in his glass.

"I will contact Sir Avery first thing in the morning," he said as he had obviously been directed to do so, yet not at all pleased about it. I sensed there was more.

"It was good that ye took Lily back to Sussex Square," he said again. "It would probably be best for ye to go there as well, then Sir Avery's people and I will see what can be learned at St. Mary's Church."

This was a new tactic—compliment, confuse, then subtly persuade.

Two could play this game, I thought, as I set my own glass on the desk. I'd had enough of stale biscuits, whisky, and a bloody stubborn Scot!

I rose from the chair across from him at the desk and went to the door to the adjacent bedroom.

"Perhaps," I replied.

It was much later when he entered the bedroom and I listened as he removed his boots, shirt, and trousers, then felt the bed dip as he joined me and pulled the blankets over the both of us.

And then, not one to easily concede, "Ye know I'm right."

I didn't respond. Instead, I kept my breathing slow and even as if I was already asleep and hadn't heard a thing he said.

He rose early the next morning, and I heard a curse from the adjacent office, then the sharp sound of the earpiece to the telephone being slammed back into the cradle.

I dressed, splashed water on my face, then joined him.

"The electric has come on," he announced. "But there's no service for the telephone." Then he looked over at me.

"It stopped snowing during the night and turned to rain. There are coaches about on the street. I will send a message to Sir Avery about the information ye found."

I'd had time to think during the night. I knew where his concern came from, even if the argument was an old one. I understood. It was not unlike my own fear for him each time he left the office to meet with someone from his time with the Metropolitan.

However...

"We can reach Hendon by rail," I announced. "There should be a train departing this morning and no difficulty with roads."

"Mikaela."

I heard the objection in his voice. Yet, I was not one to sit idly by and wait for him to return.

I pointed out that I had been part of the case from the beginning. It was through people I knew that we had learned important information, not to mention my acquaintance with members of the royal family albeit from a past case that had provided access to the Prince of Wales.

I glanced at the small watch pinned to my blouse. It was half past eight o'clock.

"The church should be open by the time we arrive."

I tucked my notebook into my bag, my fingers brushing the cold steel of the revolver Brodie insisted I carry.

He had gone into the bedroom, then returned. I was already out the door and down the stairs as the door to the office slammed shut.

"Mornin', miss," Mr. Cavendish greeted me. "That was a bit of weather earlier. We might be in for more."

"Would the messenger office have the train schedule for Hendon?" I inquired.

When there was no answer, I looked up. Brodie had arrived, and with the expression on his face, he had heard my question.

"We discussed this."

"I had no part in the discussion," I reminded him. "You

may send me off to Sussex Square, but I will go to Hendon and St. Mary's Church."

With that, I hitched up the hem of my skirt and set off across The Strand toward the messenger office. They were already open for the business of London.

"That would be King's Cross station, miss," the clerk informed me. "With a train departing at ten o'clock, if they're running on time."

I thanked him, then opened my umbrella as I stepped out onto the sidewalk, looked for a driver, and discovered Brodie had followed.

"The train departs at ten o'clock, which would be a considerably faster than going by coach." I stepped past him and waved down a driver.

"We might share the ride to King's Cross station and save the double fare," I suggested.

I didn't wait for a response but stepped up into the coach. I gave the driver the destination of the rail station. As I sat back in the seat, Brodie climbed aboard and slammed the door.

The train for Hendon was on schedule.

I purchased my own fare when we arrived. I must admit that I would not have put it past Brodie to summon a constable and have me packed off to the office or to Sussex Square. Such was the anger behind that dark gaze.

"Many of the entries in the records at St. Pancras were written in Latin," I commented as we found two seats in the main car. "It is quite common in older churches. Do you read Latin?"

Brodie shook his head. "Ye're to do exactly as I say when we arrive."

Twenty-Two

IT WAS COLD, the rain in London had turned to snow once more. Not unexpected. Though it was not far, the train to Hendon was late due to the weather.

Upon our arrival at the rail station, Brodie sent a telegram to Sir Avery explaining where we had gone and why, and that there hadn't been time earlier.

He then found a driver to take us to the church where we hoped to find more information about Reverend Chastain.

"That would be at Church End," the driver acknowledged as we stepped aboard the coach.

It was late morning when we arrived at St. Mary's church. According to the clerk at St. Pancras, there were several churches around greater London so named. Hendon was one of the oldest, dating back to the eleventh century.

It was a large church, a blend of various additions over the past eight hundred years, with a medieval tower, nave, north aisle and chapel of white-washed stone in the Gothic style.

An enormous churchyard with an arched stone entrance

and statues of two angels adjoined the building amidst a forest of cedar and yew trees.

We entered the nave and were eventually greeted by a clerk of the church. He had a studious demeanor with thinning hair and a curious but welcoming smile.

"I was certain we would have no visitors today with the weather." He introduced himself as Mr. Mannering.

"But you are more than welcome. The small chapel is always open."

Brodie handed him one of our calling cards and explained that we were looking for information about a man who once served as vicar of the church.

"I see," Mr. Mannering replied, somewhat curious by the expression at his face.

"Perhaps you would care to speak with the vicar. He can perhaps help you in the matter." He asked us to wait.

When he returned, he announced that Reverend Frankland would be pleased to meet with us.

"He's making the final changes to his sermon for Sunday's service," he explained as we reached a rather aged wood door with iron braces that might be found in a medieval castle, then escorted us into the reverend's office.

The vicar rose from behind a large desk with papers spread before him, a welcoming smile on his face. He was of medium height with brown hair that had just begun to turn grey, a warm gaze, and a welcoming smile.

"You have rescued me," the vicar commented after Brodie introduced both of us. "It's still not quite right, my sermon that is. There are so many things to speak on. I will come back to it later. Please be seated."

He gestured to the two chairs that sat before his desk.

"You are inquiring about a previous brother who served St. Mary's. How may I help you?"

"We are attempting to find the gentleman," Brodie explained. "Over a private matter on behalf of a client. Lady Forsythe has learned that he first served at St. Pancras after arriving in London some time ago and then took up the position as vicar here. We are hoping to learn where he might live now."

"We keep a very thorough record of all who serve," the reverend replied. "Our oldest records go back to 1073, a very long history serving the people of the parish.

"We usually have another clerk to assist with such things, but he is away attending a family matter. You are welcome to search through the records yourselves. They are in another part of the church.

"However, I will warn you that it can be tedious, particularly since most of the records are in Latin."

I was tempted to look over at Brodie but did not.

"Lady Forsythe has an understanding of the language," Brodie replied.

I smiled to myself.

St. Mary's was originally a Catholic church, then later Anglican after the Reformation. The history of it was there in faded paintings on walls of the north aisle that led from the nave.

There were images similar to those in the old part of Sussex Square, Norman knights of almost a thousand years before seen kneeling before a priest. Then other murals that told the church history.

I did not consider myself a person of faith. So much that I had seen during my travels had convinced me that faith came in many shapes and forms. Who was I to say that one belief was superior to another?

The church was quiet, with the faint echo of footsteps down the north aisle, a brief conversation overheard, then the sound of a door closing and Mr. Mannering returned. He asked us to follow him to what was called the reading room.

He laid a large leather-bound journal much the same as I had seen at St. Pancras on a reading stand. He then turned on a reading lamp.

"This does make it easier to read than by candlelight," he commented. "This should provide the information you're looking for. I am available if you have any questions."

Brodie thanked him as I opened the church register.

Church records were very often the only records of births, deaths and marriages across England for hundreds of years. Journals that my great aunt had at Sussex Square had been written by priests and other clerics from the time William of Normandy had arrived in Britain.

Now, I scanned entries of the past two hundred years for St. Mary's parish. It was tedious, even with my knowledge of the language, entries often written in faded text.

I eventually found the entry for Reverend Chastain. It was very near the date I had found that he had left St. Pancras.

"He was the vicar here for almost ten years!" I told Brodie, then looked for an entry recording where he had been sent afterward. There was none. However, I noted something else.

"He never left St. Mary's."

"What do ye mean?" Brodie asked.

He had been studying the framed paintings and documents on the adjacent wall of the reading room.

I read that last entry again.

"He never left. He died in 1877. It's entered here, and according to this, he's buried in the churchyard."

A sound echoed through the doorway, the clerk returning perhaps. Or possibly the vicar.

What did Chastain's death mean now?

From the beginning, there were few clues, except for that tragic event years before, as we attempted to find a motive for the murders.

The assumption, though difficult to believe, was that the vicar sought revenge for what happened even after all these years, with that cryptic message, *"The sins of the fathers."*

As Brodie had reminded me, the vicar was a father as well, and in his experience, not above such things.

Where did that leave us now?

I closed the church archive.

"Is it possible that Mary Chastain might be responsible?" I asked. "If she had eventually married? Or someone else is doing this for blackmail?" Even though no demand had been made.

"Aye, perhaps," Brodie replied.

That might be the answer as to motive. As for opportunity, it would not be that difficult to plan how she would take that revenge once she and her father had come to London.

And the means that it might be done?

Perhaps it is not so difficult if someone was paid enough or was given the promise of it.

A man who was tall, thick set and strong, who had found employment at Marlborough House stables weeks before, and I was certain I had seen on The Strand.

Yet, that did not answer the question about the man with the infirmity in his leg who was seen that night after the murder outside White's and whom I had glimpsed at the rail station.

Mr. Mannering had not yet returned.

"I'll find the man and let him know we are finished here, then I will meet ye at the front entrance," Brodie said then, and set off to find him.

He was gone for some time when Mr. Mannering appeared.

"Were you able to find the information you were looking for?" he inquired.

"Yes."

And *no*, I thought.

"Mr. Brodie went to thank you. We will be leaving."

"I must have missed him," he replied. "Perhaps he lost the way. I will tell him that we spoke if I see him."

Was Brodie waiting for me now at the entrance, having not found the clerk?

I thanked Mr. Mannering and asked him to thank Reverend Frankland as well. He accompanied me as we left the reading room.

"A moment, Lady Forsythe and I will accompany you, so that you do not lose your way. It seems that someone has left a door open."

A door across the hall stood ajar, cold air filling the hallway.

"Where does this lead?" I asked.

"The churchyard and the adjacent graveyard beyond."

A hallway door that was not open before. I would surely have noticed as we passed by.

Brodie had gone to tell the clerk we would be leaving, yet Mr. Mannering had not seen him. Had something drawn his attention elsewhere?

It would be just like him to go off on his own, particularly after our earlier conversation.

I thanked Mr. Mannering once more and assured him that I could find my way back to the entrance. Then, I stepped past him onto a stone path before he could close and bolt the door.

The landing had been protected from the weather by the overhang of the roof. Just beyond I discovered boot prints in the newly fallen snow.

They were a good size, the sort a gentleman might wear, and unless I missed my guess, I knew who they belonged to. I followed that trail of prints past the churchyard to the entrance of the graveyard.

As I entered the graveyard, those prints faded then disappeared altogether, the falling snow thicker as it dusted the trees and monuments of those buried there. And among them, the grave of Reverend Chastain, in what was noted in the register as the pavilion for the "Servants of God."

I found a small stone marker beside the pathway, and in the distance the vague outline of a small structure.

Elaborate headstones, simple markers, and stone vaults lined the path that I followed. At the end was a columned pavilion with a slate roof.

Graves surrounded the pavilion, some headstones adorned with Latin inscriptions, others with images of angels, along with a name and date of passing for the person buried there.

The headstone for Reverend William Chastain was among them with the year that he had died, 1877. And beside it, another headstone.

I brushed the snow from the name etched there:

Mary Chastain, beloved mother. 10 September 1892

"You cannot stop what must be done!"

The warning came from behind me.

"For her! For what they did!"

A man was there, a half dozen steps away, no more. Beside the grave of Mary Chastain.

He was of medium height, neither old nor young, dressed in black, pale hair tangled around his head, a crazed look in light blue eyes, as he slowly came toward me, bent over as if holding himself against some pain, his steps slow as he dragged one foot.

A man with a limp, seen after one of the murders, then briefly glimpsed through the crowd of passengers at the rail station.

"I followed you to Cambridge. You know what they did," he whispered.

I wanted to ask who he was, but it was there on Mary Chastain's gravestone—beloved mother—and evident in the way he glanced down at it now with sadness and some other emotion that narrowed his eyes as he looked back at me.

"Lady Forsythe!"

The way he said it was filled with contempt and pain as he continued to slowly move toward me.

"What she went through. All these years living with the shame of it and not even a name that any of them would give her! I have no name!

"I am nothing, but a cripple, dirt beneath their feet!"

The words were filled with pain and anger.

"No one would help her! Not any of them! And now you come here for them! To ease their guilt? I will not let you! No one can help you! Just as there was no one to help her!"

His shoulder caught me in my shoulder as he lunged at me, my bag with the revolver thrown to the ground.

He was surprisingly strong, and I was spun around, his arm clamped across my shoulders, the edge of a knife cold against my throat as I clawed at that arm and fought for footing in the mud and snow.

"Let her go."

It came from behind us, my attacker's breath hot against my cheek. And that faint scent I had smelled before.

Incense that someone might burn, the thought came and then slipped away as I continued to struggle.

That arm tightened, and I was pulled back, away from those words and a man who stepped out of the shadows of the pavilion and slowly followed, his revolver aimed at us.

"Let her go, now," Brodie repeated as he stalked us.

I was dragged backward, that blade at my throat, as I stared at Brodie and the slow but deliberate way he moved as the son of Mary Chastain limped haltingly, taking me with him.

"She had no part in what happened all those years before," Brodie told him. "Just as those young men had nothing to do with it."

"You don't know. You don't understand!" the man with that knife screamed.

"I do know," Brodie said then in that same calm voice as he took another step toward us.

"I found my own mother butchered and left for dead as a lad. I know what it is to have something taken from ye that ye can never get back."

"No!" the man at my back screamed. "It has to be done. The sins of the fathers. An eye for an eye!"

Through the snow that had begun to fall once more, I saw shadows that moved through the trees. He must have seen as well as they moved closer.

I felt a sharp prick of pain as that blade pressed against my neck, the knife cold. And something far colder in the expression on Brodie's face.

The sharp report of the revolver shattered the silence, smoke exploding in the air as he came toward us, then fired again, and again.

The man behind me staggered, then fell backwards and I was pulled down with him into the cold snow.

I fought and screamed, clawing to free myself of that arm and the weight of that body, those pale blue eyes of Mary Chastain's son staring at me.

Brodie pulled me to my feet.

I was covered in mud, bloodied, and shaking.

"Bloody hell!"

There might have been another curse, but it was muffled by the front of his coat as Brodie pulled me against him.

"Is he dead?"

His beard was soft against my cheek, as those other shadows I had glimpsed only moments before emerged from the trees and rushed toward us.

"Aye."

Epilogue

TWO DAYS LATER, THE STRAND, LONDON

"I AM PLEASED that you were not seriously injured, Lady Forsythe." Sir Avery rose from the chair across the desk from Brodie.

That could be subject to one's perspective, I thought.

The cut I had received in that attack in the graveyard at St. Mary's had been well bandaged by Mr. Brimley upon our return to London late that same night after we'd met with the local police. The bandage was bothersome, and I had since removed it.

The director of the Special Services Agency had received Brodie's telegram and was responsible for the arrival of the Metropolitan Police at St. Mary's, those *"shadows"* I had seen in the tree cover just beyond the graveyard.

A great deal has been learned in the past two days since the attack.

William Chastain, so named after his grandfather, Reverend William Chastain, was the man who had attacked me and was responsible for three murders and the attack on the Duke of York.

He had been born after Reverend Chastain and his daughter arrived in London. There was a record of it in the later entries at St. Pancras church where Reverend Chastain served as vicar.

From subsequent records that were found, Mary Chastain had never married, her son born out of wedlock.

She had lived with her father near St. Pancras and had continued to live with him until his death from illness. She continued to live near St. Mary's Church, his final position, on the small pension he received and what she earned as a lady's maid and at a local tavern.

The tall, heavyset man who had aided her son had been caught and arrested after the attack on the Duke of York. He had provided information about where he had met with William Chastain and where Chastain lived in a single room at a tenement in Spitalfields after the death of his mother.

He had no doubt eventually asked to know who his father was, as children were wont to do. There was no answer because she could not name him after that night at the tavern near Cambridge.

He had apparently been born with the lameness in one leg, noted by the physician in Hendon after the attack in the churchyard.

How he had learned the circumstances of his birth could only be speculated upon. Perhaps Mary Chastain had finally spoken of it on her deathbed to unburden herself. However, the two people who knew the truth of that were now both dead.

The neck scarf Lily had found was much like those worn by the vicars of the Church. Had Mary Chastain's son attempted to wrap himself in the cloth of the righteous, as Brodie had suggested? That would remain unknown.

As for the marks that had been made on each victim's body, perhaps a crude image of a cross, meant to be a symbol of absolution for a sinner?

So much that would never be known for certain.

The Prince of Wales had been informed that the case had been resolved with the threat ended. Not surprising there was no mention in the daily newspaper the day after, nor today.

I had sent a note the day before, as promised, to Lady Walsingham. I briefly explained that the case had concluded, and the person responsible for her son's murder was dead. I had received a note in response just this morning that simply read —*Thank you.*

Perhaps there was some comfort to be had in the knowledge that the man had been found and was now dead.

I would call on her when it was appropriate, as I liked her very much.

After Sir Avery left, Brodie stepped to the cabinet and poured us both a dram of whisky.

He handed a tumbler to me and slowly sipped from his own glass.

Not a man of many words or grand gestures, still he reached out and lightly brushed his fingers near the cut on my neck.

"Ye should have left the bandage on a day or two more."

Care and concern in a comment about wound care.

How could a woman possibly resist such words? The truth was that I could not.

However...

I took a sip of whisky. It was warm, with just a hint of heather; earthy, musky, and slightly floral, with hints of honey and lavender, according to Mr. Hutton who oversaw the distilling of it at Old Lodge in the north of Scotland.

"There is one part of the case that we have not yet discussed," I commented.

That dark gaze was a bit distracting.

"What might that be?"

"You fired three shots when one obviously was sufficient." I added. "The physician was quite certain of it after he examined the body."

He took another sip of whisky, that dark gaze warm as the color of the drink in his hand.

I waited as he emptied the tumbler, then reached out, his fingers gentle on my cheek, that dark gaze, darker still.

A man I could trust.

Author Note

So many changes were coming about as the end of the 19th century approached.

The London railway system had expanded considerably, and the London Tube actually opened in 1863 on a very limited basis, with the Metropolitan Railway between Paddington and Farringdon. An electric line opened for service in 1890 between the city and the South London Railway.

For the story, Mikaela and Lily traveled from London to Cambridge on the steam rail line from King's Cross Station.

There were numerous well-known scandals surrounding the Prince of Wales, from his early university days and throughout his life.

I've used an incident at Trinity College at Cambridge that necessitated a visit from Prince Albert. The young Prince Edward Albert subsequently left Trinity for military service and travel abroad. I have expanded upon that incident for the basis of the story. The names of the victims and their families are fictitious, although I have used some well-known historical persons in addition to the Prince of Wales.

Edward Albert, who would eventually assume the throne after the death of his mother, Queen Victoria, was the second son. His older brother, who would normally have succeeded, died the year before from influenza.

London newspapers were rampant with scandals, however there was censorship in certain situations which figured into the story as well, and makes the inquiry case all the more difficult for Brodie and Mikaela.

The gentleman's club, White's, has a long history in London society, one of those places barred to women and where men could indulge in...entertainments.

A lift has now been installed at the office on The Strand, making travel from the street to the office more convenient, although not without some complications, as demonstrated by Rupert the hound.

The Jampot is a real coffeehouse tucked into a small courtyard off Cornhill. In the story, it's where Brodie goes to meet with Mr. Dooley at the beginning of the case.

According to my research, there are in excess of a dozen St. Mary's parish churches in greater London. I've used two of them for Deadly Murder.

Church archives and records were written in Latin for centuries and at the time of the story. Most are now written in English.

As for Lily... She is no longer a child, a fact Mikaela is forced to accept. Along the way, she has discovered how intelligent and impulsive she is, not to mention possibly a little too worldly for her own good. And then, there is the obvious tension between Lily and Munro yet to be explored...

Thank you for reading. And next...Angus Brodie and Mikaela Forsythe Murder Mystery Book 15—DEADLY REVENGE.

Also by Carla Simpson

Angus Brodie and Mikaela Forsythe Murder Mystery

A Deadly Affair

Deadly Secrets

A Deadly Game

Deadly Illusion

A Deadly Vow

Deadly Obsession

A Deadly Deception

A Deadly Betrayal

A Deadly Scandal

Deadly Lies

Deadly Curse

Deadly Ghost

Deadly Attraction

Deadly Murder

Merlin Series

Daughter of Fire

Daughter of the Mist

Daughter of the Light

Shadows of Camelot

Dawn of Camelot

Daughter of Camelot

The Young Dragons, Blood Moon

Clan Fraser

Betrayed

Revenge

Outlaws, Scoundrels & Lawmen

Desperado's Caress

Passion's Splendor

Silver Mistress

Memory and Desire

Desire's Flame

Silken Surrender

Angels, Devils, Rebels & Rogues

Ravished

Always My Love

Seductive Caress

Seduced

Deceived

About the Author

"I want to write a book ..." she said.

"Then do it," he said.

And she did, and received two offers for that first book proposal.

A dozen historical romances later, and a prophecy from a gifted psychic and the Legacy Series was created, expanding to seven additional titles.

Along the way, two film options, and numerous book awards.

But wait, there's more a voice whispered, after a trip to Scotland and a visit to the standing stones in the far north, and as old as Stonehenge, sign posts the voice told her, and the Clan Fraser books that have followed that told the beginnings of the clan and the family she was part of ...

And now ... murder and mystery set against the backdrop of Victorian London in the new Angus Brodie and Mikaela Forsythe series, with an assortment of conspirators and murderers in the brave new world after the Industrial Revolution where terrorists threaten and the world spins closer to war.

When she is not exploring the Darkness of the fantasy world, or pursuing ancestors in ancient Scotland, she lives in the mountains near Yosemite National Park with bears and mountain lions, and plots murder and revenge.

And did I mention fierce, beautiful women and dangerous, handsome men?

They're there, waiting ...

Join Carla's Newsletter